The wise want love; and those who love want wisdom;
And all best things are thus confused with ill.
                                        —Shelley

A Different Love

a gay romance by
Clay Larkin

Boston: Alyson Publications, Inc.

A Different Love is published as a paperback original by Alyson Publications, Inc., PO Box 2783, Boston, MA 02208. Distributed in Great Britain by Gay Men's Press, PO Box 247, London, N15 6RW.

Manufactured in the United States of America.

First edition, first printing: August 1983.

ISBN 0 932870 37 6

To "Frank,"
wherever he may be

1

In San Francisco, California Street is the main thoroughfare from the grandeur and elegance of Nob Hill to the hang-loose gay scene along Polk Gulch. Wide and marked by silvery cable car tracks, it descends gently for half a mile between high, unbroken walls of bay-windowed apartment houses.

At the top of the hill, where there are views of the city and the bay, the rents are high. Down by Polk Street many of the buildings show the wear and tear of the transient population. The neighborhood between is fairly quiet, middle-class, and more than a little gay. In this area, in a bedroom of a second-floor flat, two young men lay together, in the night-time darkness, deep in each other's embrace. Their hold grew tighter as they shuddered with the ecstacy of approaching climax. One of the men suddenly groaned, the other emitted a sharp sigh....

After a while their bodies relaxed, and they lay side by side, still half-embracing and breathing hard. One of the men was fairly tall, dark-haired, and heavily muscled. The other was shorter and well proportioned but a little thin. What light there was in the room seemed to be concentrated in his mass of straight blond hair.

He brushed a strand of it aside and said, "I'm so happy, Harold, thanks to you."

"You make me pretty damn happy too," his lover replied, a deep but quiet voice gently rumbling out the words. "You're glad we came to San Francisco?"

"Yes! Very glad."

"Me too. I guess most of the hassles are over with. When I think of all the problems and ugly stuff we left behind, it seems to me that we did just the right thing."

"Of course it was, Hal, darling," the blond man said. He lay quietly for a few moments, but something came to mind, and he went on: "Maybe this is silly, but everything feels just so right, I wish we could celebrate."

"I guess we can, Billy, but how?"

"Well. . . ."

"Come on, tell me."

"Hal, I know it's a week night, but I've been twenty-one for almost a month, and it isn't that late, and we did talk about going to some gay bars when we got settled."

Harold could not help but smile at his fair-haired lover lying beside him in the dark. "We're about as settled as we're going to get. And it isn't all that late. I reckon we can go have a couple of beers somewhere." He reached a big arm over Billy and switched on the bedside lamp. "You're the one who arranged everything. Remember where you put the gay guidebook?"

"I know exactly," Billy said as he lept from the bed.

Harold sat up against the pillows and gazed at his lover as he rummaged through the chest of drawers on the far side of the bedroom. Even now, after a double dose of sex and his intimate acquaintance with every inch of Billy's body, Harold felt a certain ache in his throat. How wonderful that anyone so charming and so beautiful could be his. How great that they could communicate so well across the eleven-year gap in their ages. Billy was naive, yes, and impulsive, but gorgeous as well, inside and out.

Harold never tired of looking at Billy, at his hair that flowed like water and ranged in a thousand tints of color from tawny to straw, and at his face. It was lightly tanned and graced with two startling eyes of deep blue. Harold admired almost as highly the lithe, sleek, well-defined body that moved with a quickness possessed only by the very young.

"I found it!" Billy said. He turned, came rushing, and jumped onto the bed.

Harold grabbed his naked lover by his middle to keep him from bouncing to the floor. When the laughing and hugging were done, Billy opened the thick little book.

"Gee," he said, "there's pages and pages of listings for San Francisco."

"Look for places on California Street."

"Yes... Let's see. There's a place on California near Arguello, and—"

"That's awful far away," Harold said.

"Oh, wait. The Beacon! That's the little bar right across the street!"

"Really? I guess I've passed it a dozen times and didn't even guess."

"Come on," Billy said, "Let's go take a look."

Harold agreed easily, hiding his nervousness. In his thirty-two years he had visted only one gay bar, and that had been a long time ago. He had been Billy's age and curious. Shortly after that he had decided to suppress certain disturbing impulses in himself and get married. Now, though, Billy's wishes were Harold's commands. He didn't want Billy to realize this and become spoiled, but Harold knew that there was very little he could deny his blue-eyed young lover.

The Beacon was in a corner building, and its walls, front and side, were all windows. Unusual for gay bars in most of the country, this openness was a recent trend in San Fransisco, and the sight of soft lights glowing on redwood gave a warm, pleasant picture to the passerby.

The barroom was fairly wide and quite deep; its furnishings and illumination had been arranged to create the illusion of intimacy.

The Beacon's barback, an ornate, handsome piece of Victoriana in cherrywood and brass, rose high and wide behind Frank, the bartender. He was finding it a very slow shift, even with his friend Warren for company. "Hey, Warren," he called out from down the bar, where he was washing glasses, "When are we going to make it?"

His friend, remarkably good looking with curly dark red hair and light brown eyes, answered in a suave baritone, "Saving it for my wedding night."

"Hell, I'll marry you," Frank replied. "Do you cook and sew and swab toilets and all that?"

"Nope. Just decorative."

Frank thought of Warren as a lot more than that. Warren had been coming into the bar for almost a year now and with great regularity — quietly amusing, ironic and a bit cynical, but friendly and very sexy. All Frank's efforts at getting him into bed, however, had gone nowhere. Bit by bit the bartender figured out that his favorite customer and pleasant friend did not want to have a relationship with anyone: Warren had lead an extremely wild sex life for years, then had tired of it all. Nowadays all he did was drop into some bathhouse a couple of times a week for fast-food sex.

Frank knew too that Warren was thirty-five to his own forty years, and that if the handsome redhead ever chose to have a serious relationship again it might well be with a man nearer his own age or younger, not with someone five years older.

The bartender noticed two newcomers who had just entered the nearly empty Beacon bar. They were standing just inside the entrance and nervously gazing about.

Straight tourists, Frank thought, who've stumbled into the wrong place.

The pair, one tall, big and darkhaired, the other shorter, thin and blond, sat down on adjoining stools at the bar and ordered beers.

Frank served them after checking the younger man's identification. From down the bar a way he noticed that they drank in silence and kept staring around the room. Frank began to wonder if they planned to cause some kind of trouble. Replenishing the garnish tray as an excuse to be near them, he casually asked, "You guys new in town?"

"Oh no," Harold said. "We've been here a while."

"A month," Billy added. "Before that we lived in this hotel on Market Street which wasn't bad or anything, you know, but it sure was, well, kind of grim. But this part of town is neat. We didn't even know this bar was here, until we found it in our gay guidebook. We can see it out our front window, in fact."

Frank relaxed, smiled a little and asked, "Come from back East?"

"Eastern Iowa," Billy said. "We had to leave. It was actually kind of romantic. . . to look back on. Not at the time though."

Harold didn't like his lover talking so openly about their lives to a stranger, even if this bartender did seem friendly. "You make us sound like criminals, Billy." Turning back to Frank he said, "Word got out about us, and. . . well, we wanted to leave anyway."

"We knew San Francisco would be a place we could live together without any problems," Billy said.

If Harold felt uneasy about Billy giving out personal information, he was glad his young lover thought it had all been so simple. For Harold their problem had been immense and painful and complicated. But then, he had to admit to himself that he brought a lot of problems along from the years before Billy came into his life. In his early twenties Harold had married, and for over ten years he had not let himself look twice at an attractive man. At work he had kept his head down and done his job. At home he had labored to find reasons to love his wife. She discovered after a few years that she was unable to have children, became bitter, and blamed him for her misfortune.

Finally they had taken to sleeping in separate rooms. His wife had said that his snoring kept her awake, a complaint that she had never made before. For Harold their sex life was no great loss; it had been pleasant enough but never ecstatic. He returned to masturbation, and now he let his mind-pictures run free and uncensored. His imagining of the bodies and ways of men were the only distractions he had from his dully unhappy life.

For his coworkers at the foundry the remedy for an imperfect marriage seemed to be found in the tavern with a few after-work beers and a few laughs with the guys, or maybe more than a few beers. Harold didn't want to add that kind of dreariness to his already depressing existence, so he took to walking home. It was a long journey but invigorating, and it effectively cut down on the time that he'd have to spend with his wife, not that she ever seemed to mind his absence anymore.

One early evening in the spring, when Harold was walking home through slush that lay everywhere, a young man flew past him on a bicycle. A few yards ahead the five-speed leaped into the air and sent its rider crashing head first to the pavement. Harold had run over to the young man and helped him to his feet, asking "You okay?"

"I think so... yeah. Thanks, mister. Oh, hell, it looks like my wheel is bent. Guess I hit a rock or something under the snow."

The young blond man picked up his crippled bicycle.

"You walking up Elm?" Harold asked, trying not to stare, trying to avoid staring at the beautiful face and dark blue eyes. "I'll help carry your bike a ways."

"Great. I live just three blocks up. Hey, my name is Billy."

When they reached a modest wooden house, Billy invited Harold to get warm, insisting he have a can of beer. As they drank Billy explained his father had disappeared years before and that his mother worked evenings as a hostess in a steak house. Then he became an insistent blond young animal. Harold let himself be seduced. He had never experienced such pleasure in his life, never in marriage, and not in the few furtive experiments he'd made with men, years before.

Still, Harold was bothered, and he realized that it showed on his face when Billy said, "Don't feel bad. I thought I was terrible too, when I started four months ago, but I sent off to this gay organization for some pamphlets, and I read that it's all very natural. I've got them right here. Take them with you, read them."

"Well... all right," Harold said. "When can I bring them back?"

"Tomorrow," Billy answered. "With or without the pamphlets. Will you?"

"Umm... I — Yes. I'll come by after work... if that's okay with you."

"Great," Billy whooped. More quietly he said, "Maybe then you'll tell me your name."

"It's Harold... Call me Hal." He smiled. The two men shook hands.

The next day and almost every day after work Harold went to see Billy. He found out that the young man was almost twenty, had plans for college but not the money, and was working in a retail auto parts store. "Mom'll help me all she can, but basically I've gotta make it through college on my own."

After six months of this Harold's wife began to wonder about his life outside their home. When she accused him of having an affair with Billy's mother, Harold knew that she must have had him followed. "And I talked to her on the phone today and said I'd make lots of trouble if it didn't stop."

Harold became so angry he thought he was going to commit murder. Billy's mother had been tolerant and understanding, even going to far as to say she prefered a nice steady adult in Billy's life to a lot of the kids his own age. However, her tolerance stretched only so far: after the third or fourth phone call from Harold's increasingly hateful wife, Billy's mother counterblasted with the truth.

In a way Harold was glad. The inevitable break would come all the sooner. To avoid exposure and alimony he signed over everything to his wife and moved across town into an apartment with Billy. Harold's ex-wife was not as discreet as she might have been about it; soon more and more of the men at work began to avoid him. One day he had a near-miss accident. The beam that came crashing down inches away from him could have gotten loose by error, but on the other hand....

When the front door of the apartment was firebombed, an amateurish job that did little damage, their elderly, frightened landlady asked them to move out as soon as they could.

"Let's leave this town completely," Billy said. "I can go to college anywhere. Can you get a foundry job anywhere else?"

"Very likely. But...."

"But what?"

"Nothing, I guess," Harold sighed. "Now that I think about it I can't see any reason to stay here. Where'll we go, Dubuque?"

"Well, I was thinking of a city a little farther away. How about San Francisco?"

"San Francisco?"

"Don't look so amazed, Hal. We'll love it. Nobody cares if you're gay out there. I can go to school, get a part-time job, you can work, and after I finish college we could maybe set up some kind of little business together."

Though his bitterness was great, Harold had found it strangely difficult to leave the town where he had been born and raised. But Billy's enthusiasm was catching. The problems of ending one life and beginning another once had seemed unending, but now, he felt, they had been solved, and he thought he could get and give more and greater love then he had ever known. Here they were, settled in this beautiful city, and now they had found a pleasant bar where they could have a drink from time to time.

So they're lovers, and kind of new to all this, Frank thought as he worked behind the bar. Wouldn't mind getting it on with the big guy. Massive, butch, and gentle, what a great combination. But he's crazy about that thin, pretty kid, so... way it goes.

A new customer came in, and Frank went down the bar to take his order. He knew the man's name was Deek Jameson but did not greet him, though Jameson was a fairly frequent patron of the Beacon. Frank had long felt an instinctive dislike for him and now as always he covered it with a bland neutrality, knowing his job was to be a bartender, not a judge of men's lives. But he knew the many stories told him by the good-looking young men, about how the fifty-ish Deek dazzled them with wealth and charm, then discarded them for the next pretty youth. Frank had heard other stories too, concerning young men who made Deek their victim — apparently he reveled in the humiliations they created for him.

When Billy and Harold got up and said their shy, smiling goodnights, Frank smiled back, waved, and watched them leave, all the while admiring Harold's huge, well-set shoulders. He watched as the two men started across California Street and, taking each others hand, begin to giggle at doing such a daring thing in public.

Frank smiled again and turned back to his work. Warren's observant eyes met his, and they both grinned. No doubt Warren had seen them too.

In a short time Deek Jameson called for another drink. Frank brought it to him, and Jameson asked about the young blond man.

"First time I saw him in here," Frank said, and moved down to the back corner of the bar where Warren was in his usual place, ideal for seeing almost all that went on in the Beacon.

"Nice guys," Frank said.

"Tourists?"

"Nope. Just moved here from the Midwest. Case of true love."

Warren slowly shook his head. "Of all the places in the world for a couple of hicks to bring their true love... San Francisco is a good place to go wild, not steady."

"Voice of authority?" Frank asked.

"Experience."

"Well, yeah, Warren, you could give an advanced college course in being jaded." Slightly irritated, Frank went on, speaking with the leeway allowed between friends: "You came to the city to go wild, and that's what you did for ten or fifteen years. And sure, when a guy's real young, hot sex is the whole trip. But man, you're, well...."

"Thirty-five if I'm a day, Frank... But do go on with your self-improvement lecture."

"Nah. It's just that, like, you wouldn't be bored and you wouldn't assume that it's impossible for two guys to be lovers in this town, if you could let yourself care for somebody. Then you'd really see what you're missing. It's like, well, just plain sex without any feeling can be fun and all, but in the long run it's like someone singing a beautiful song very well, you know, getting all the notes right and everything, but not having much emotion behind it. The song doesn't come across, doesn't mean very much."

"It's more fun when you care?" Warren asked, voice edged with sarcasm."

"Exactly."

"Frank, my dear friend and old buddy, I may be jaded, but you are definitely old enough to know better. Two people can fall in love, sure, but it sure helps if they are located where there aren't too many sexual distractions or temptations. I'll bet you that pair tonight, mad

14

as they are about each other, or as they think they are, won't last a month."

"Sure they will," Frank said.

"Not in San Francisco. I'll bet you ten dollars."

"You're on, but how will we know?"

"They went into that white apartment building across the street," Warren said, "so maybe they'll hang out here, and maybe we can find out what's what."

"Okay," said Frank. "You're going to lose though. I can tell the real thing when I see it. Those two are crazy about each other." Frank had a sudden thought, which he put into words: "If I lose I'll pay the ten bucks. But if I win, you don't pay me a penny. You give me a night of sex, inside of, say, seventy-two hours after the bet's settled. Can you go for that?"

Warren broke into his sleepy, knowing smile and brushed a hand through his thick, dark red hair. *So Frank wants to take me to bed and show me what real love is all about. Frank the do-gooder, something new to me. Well, he does have a big heart down below that large mouth of his.*

"We just observe?" Warren asked. "No twiddling the dials of their lives, or telling them about the bet or anything like that?"

"Right."

"And all the information has to come from them, one or the other or both. No second-hand gossip stuff?"

"Sure."

They shook hands.

Warren took a sip of his drink, then said, "There's just one thing. I mean, I'm no kid and not to be vain, but is my ass worth only ten dollars?"

Frank parried, "How the hell should I know? I haven't had it yet."

Warren smiled and finished his drink. "I've got to go. Must be down in the Financial District at the crack of dawn." He stood up. "You know, I'd just as soon lose the bet, in one sense. I wish those guys well. But this is San Francisco, sex on every corner, and those two are both good looking and hot, especially the little blond. He's a knock-out."

"You'll see," Frank said. "A month from now you'll discover what real affection is all about."

"Sure," Warren said. "Good night."

Warren walked up California Street in the cool darkness of early summer, heading toward his nearby apartment. Idly he wondered about Frank as a sex partner: Italian, nice looking, big dark eyes, lightly olive complexion, hair black and full, a little wavy, and coarse, a solid body, wiry and compact. Not bad, not bad at all. Of course, he had had butch, handsome, hairy-chested Italian types before. . . .

A little stab of fear struck, and Warren wondered why he should worry about the prospect of losing this wager. What would be so terrible about making it with Frank? It would be just another trick. That's all it would be. But then, Warren well knew, with his years of experience, he always found it more pleasant to have a one night stand with a stranger then with a friend. No complications that way. . . .

2

Billy and Harold started across California Street, heading for the Beacon Bar. As they approached they could see that the place was crowded, full of men standing and sitting everywhere, under the warm glow of the antique lamps and brass chandelier.

Harold led the way inside and Billy followed in his wake. Toward the back they claimed a table that was just being vacated.

Billy went up to the bar. He found two bartenders at work and moved a few feet to be sure to have service from Frank.

"Hey, Billy. How are you guys doing?"

"Just fine, Frank," he answered, pleased to be remembered.

"What'll it be?"

Billy ordered two beers and watched the smooth way Frank swung around the cooler and returned with two gleaming brown bottles, removed the caps, and set the beers on the counter where they were quickly joined by two napkins and two glasses. When Frank returned from the register with the change he asked Billy, "Where's your friend?"

"Harold? Over there, at the table."

"Oh, yeah." Frank waved and Harold waved back. Then he put the glasses over the necks of the bottles, said "Good to see you guys again," and moved up the bar to another customer.

Billy felt many eyes gazing at him as he made his way through the crowd. Somebody gave his ass a brief but firm grope. He was amused but reached the table and his lover with a sense of relief.

One of the men observing Billy was Warren, seated at his usual vantage point towards the back of the bar. He thought that the young man, with his classical good looks, big blue eyes and appealing mouth, would be desired by any number of men but especially by those who liked their love objects to be rather naive and somewhat boyish in manner. Yes, Billy would have many admirers here in the city, Warren knew, Billy's friend appealed to another taste, to men who liked ruggedness, a strong air of adult masculinity, and muscles. Warren reflected that there was a big market for that kind of man too. Yes, it would only be a matter of time. . . .

Harold gazed quietly across the table at Billy, glad to see him excited and happy, pleased that Billy's twenties would be much more pleasurable than his own had been.

"You're staring at me," Billy said quietly.

"Guess I am. Good to see you enjoying yourself."

"You're so quiet, Hal. Tired from work?"

"Nope. Feel great. What'll we do tomorrow?"

"The laundry?" Billy asked.

"I mean for fun."

"But I *love* doing the laundry," said Billy, miming a huge yawn.

"I was thinking of maybe a trip out to Golden Gate Park."

"Oh, yes! Let's. Been here over a month and haven't seen Golden Gate Park. I mean, what kind of San Franciscans are we?"

As Harold started to reply, his beer bottle suddenly began to dance, stumbled at the edge of the table, and fell to the floor. Billy grabbed his bottle, but the beer slopped out of the nearly full glass and fanned across the table top.

"Oh! I am sorry."

They looked up to find an older man standing there. He was dressed in a well-tailored white summer suit, pink shirt and dark red tie.

"Somebody bumped into me, and I'm afraid I—"

"That's okay," said Harold amiably.

"By no means. Allow me to replace your drinks."

The man waved his hand, and in a few moments a young man came

18

up. He wore a white apron tight around his waist. After swabbing the table dry, he took an order for two beers and a gin and tonic.

"He'll be right back," the man said. "Would you mind if I sat down for a moment?"

"Please," Harold replied; he felt slightly uneasy but aware he could say little else under the circumstances.

In the introductions that followed the man gave his name as Deek Jameson, and with charm, tact, and sympathy he got Harold and Billy to talk about themselves.

"So you plan to develop a business together. Well, I think that's a very nice idea."

"Well, not for a few years," Harold said.

"I have to get through college," Billy added.

"Oh. Of course. Well, I must go." Jameson stood up, drink in hand. "It's been so pleasant talking to you both."

"Equally, Mr. Jameson," Harold said.

"Do call me Deek. I come in here often, live just up the hill. Good night."

When Deek had disappeared in the crowd Billy said, "I bet he has his clothes made, and if he lives at the top of the hill, that must mean Nob Hill. He must be rich."

"Could be," Harold said.

Frank's voice reached them, strong and loud: "Last call!"

"I didn't think that it was so late," Billy said.

"Me neither. Drink up and we'll go home."

In a short time they were moving through the thinning crowd, heading for the front door. As they were about to step out onto California Street, Deek Jameson came up to them. "Harold, Billy, I'm having a few friends over for a little after-hours party. Why don't you join us? I live quite nearby."

Billy and Harold both spoke at once, and Harold's slow words of excuse were lost under Billy's lighthearted reply, "Oh, we'd love to. Right, Harold?"

"Well, sure... for a little while."

Jameson asked if they had a car.

"No," Billy said. "We live across the street."

"Well then, come with me. My car is outside."

Jameson waved to some friends and left with Billy and Harold and a well-dressed young man with wavy dark hair and a beautiful catlike face. He was introduced as Jeffrey and greeted Harold and Billy with the barest politeness.

19

Deek's large black automobile came around the corner. A man wearing a black cape got out of it and opened the door on the curb side.

The richly upholstered interior was silver and grey, and to Billy the view of California Street was far more glamorous now than when he was on foot.

Back inside the Beacon, which was almost empty, Warren said to a busy Frank, "I don't know if you saw our dream couple, but...."

"I know they were here."

"Well, Jameson moved in on them, and he just snagged them as they were going out the door, for a drink somewhere, I guess."

"So? They're still together, still a couple."

"True, but you better get that ten bucks ready."

Frank looked up, grinned at Warren and said, "You better start loosening your belt."

Suddenly breaking into a smile, Warren swung off the bar stool and said, "I'm not so worried. Good night, Frank."

On top of Nob Hill the limousine made a slow, heavy turn off California Street, passed the huge Gothic bulk of Grace Cathedral, and in a block or two came to a halt in front of a tall building.

A doorman let them into a marble-walled lobby, and an elevator took the party to the top floor. Its doors parted to reveal a beautifully furnished room. Billy was enchanted. Harold felt uncomfortable. The group of men went through a doorway into a huge living room, and Billy was amazed to realize that the first room had been merely a foyer.

He was impressed as well with the living room. Its north and east walls were glass from floor to ceiling, revealing a vast amount of San Francisco — Russian Hill, North Beach, the Financial District, and the bay, black and gleaming in the night.

Other men arrived and came into the living room, settling on one of the several islands of couch and chairs. Jameson took drink orders himself. "Scotch for me," Billy said.

Harold knew Billy had drunk very little hard liquor in his life and suspected his lover was trying to live up to Jameson's style of life.

"With water? On the rocks? Or straight up?"

"On the rocks," Billy said. It sounded better than having it with water, and he wasn't exactly sure what "straight up" meant.

In a short time the cat-faced young man brought their drinks on a tray. Their thanks were met with a mechanical smile.

All around them men were talking in groups and bunches. Harold smelled marijuana smoke. The chitchat was full of names he didn't know, shows he hadn't seen, scandals he didn't understand. And the style of the conversation was not straightforward as he liked, but an odd, mocking banter.

Billy too felt himself to be an outsider, but he was more fascinated than bothered by the scene.

Harold told Billy, "I'm going to look at the view."

"I'll stay here," Billy replied, wanting to hear the end of a racy story about a famous politician.

Harold found his way through arrangements of furniture to the northeast corner of the room where two windows met. He stood gazing out at the city's lights, wanting to be at home, lying with Billy's thin body snug against his, sharp little shoulder blades against his chest, and falling asleep in the pleasure of Billy's warmth and soft male odor.

Music started up far across the room, and Harold saw in the window's reflection that men were dancing together. He hoped that Billy wouldn't want to dance with him. He did not know how to dance with a man and was embarrassed by the idea.

A man came up to where Billy was sitting and asked him to dance. Billy politely refused. He had never danced with a man in his life. The couples did make it look very easy though, and Billy wished he and Harold had practiced dancing together. But they'd never thought of doing that, and Hal, Billy was sure, would never want to try. He comforted himself with the thought that they might look like a study in comical contrasts if they were on the dance floor together.

Feeling alone, Billy got up to join his lover at the windows.

"Billy, there you are," Deek Jameson said. "Come, let me show you my little garden."

"A garden?"

"Yes indeed. Come this way."

Billy followed his host across the room and through a door. Beyond a large kitchen another door let them out into the night air. Jameson turned a switch and strong lights came on, revealing a little square of greenery, some tubs of ornamental plants, and white-painted wrought-iron lawn chairs with a matching picnic table.

"Wow...."

"You like it?"

"It's fantastic. This whole place is."

Moving closer and speaking softly, Jameson said, "The kitchen windows are too high for the help to see out, and the only other ones,

21

over there, are those of a guest bedroom, which usually is empty. This is an ideal place to get lots of sun. You must feel free to use it when you want a suntan... any time. If I'm not at home the houseboy will let you in."

"He will? I mean, that's very nice of you."

Billy took a big sip of his scotch, feeling rather nervous and noticing that Jameson was looking at him rather intently. The liquor burned his throat as it went down. "Well, I better get back to Harold."

"Of course," Jameson said: "This way."

Back in the living room they found that only one man was dancing. The music was Ravel's *Bolero*, the man was Jeffrey, Jameson's feline-looking friend, and he was naked.

Once more amazed, Billy stopped and stared. The feverish music reached its dissonant, shimmering climax and came to the abrupt end. At this point the dancer threw himself to the blue and white oriental carpet, directly in front of Deek Jameson.

Everyone applauded, and Billy found Harold, still over at the corner of the room, gazing out the windows.

"Hi. Just saw Deek's little garden, it's hidden in the middle of the place, sort of like the hole in the doughnut."

"I'm very tired," Harold said.

"Well, we better go," Billy responded, sure that Harold had been shocked by the nude dancer.

Harold knew that Billy didn't want to leave, but who could say what was coming next at this 'party'?

They found Jameson and said goodnight. He offered to have the driver take them home, but Harold politely said they lived very near-by and would walk.

Outside, as they went down California Street, Billy said, "That was really something. I didn't think anyone really lived like that — like in the movies."

"Mmmm," was Harold's reply.

"And his friends, they're so sophisticated... And that guy who danced, you think that he's Jameson's boyfriend?"

"I think that Jameson is keeping him," Harold said.

"Really? You don't think they love each other?"

Harold was amused to hear the mystification in Billy's voice. "Who can say? But I doubt it. There's thirty years difference in their ages, and the young man is a little too nice to Jameson to really mean it."

"Oh. Yeah, I guess," Billy said and walked for a while in silence. He was just begining to realize clearly that love didn't dominate every

22

couple relationship in the world. It was something he had known before only in a vague, abstract way, "I wonder why that Jeffrey was sort of nasty to us. We didn't do anything to him."

"Kind of ill-bred, I guess," Harold answered.

"You didn't like him dancing bare-ass, did you?"

"I didn't care."

At home they had hot, brief sex, and lay back to sleep. Billy, snuggled deep in Harold's comforting arms, thought of the gorgeous existence that Deek Jameson must lead, and he wondered about Harold: where was his curiosity about the world? Billy's own desire to know all about life was so strong that he was puzzled by his lover's lack of interest in his surroundings.

Harold half-regretted that he and Billy had sex tonight. He knew they had both been turned on by the naked exhibition of the wildly dancing Jeffrey, and that seemed a little dirtying to Harold, as if they had brought some of Jameson's way of life into their bed.

Bushed by the busy Friday night at the Beacon and facing an even busier Saturday night, Frank slept late. Just as he finished showering and shaving, the telephone rang.

"Hi, it's Larry. How's it going?"

"Hey, Larry. Long time."

"Yeah, exactly what I was thinking. Listen Frank, why don't you come up for dinner Sunday, and then... whatever?"

"Gee, Larry, I've got something lined up," Frank lied.

"Oh... I was sort of hoping we'd start seeing each other again. You know?"

Frank lied some more: "Well, I'm kind of involved with somebody right now."

"Nice. I'm really good at keeping my mouth shut. You're off Monday night, too, right? How about then?"

Prompted by the familiar voice, Frank saw a picture of Larry in his mind: early thirties, good solid body, sexy-angel kind of face. In the past he and Larry had enjoyed great sex together, but never anything else, though Frank had tried for a while to make it a fuller relationship.

"Can't," Frank said. "I'm pretty serious about this guy."

"Well, great. I'm just sorry your new friend cuts out the old ones."

"Larry, come on. We weren't friends or lovers or anything, just sex partners. Fine, but... well, nowadays, I want something more."

"I mess around, Frank. You knew that."

23

Frank felt iritated and trapped. "We want different things. I want to matter to a guy out of bed and in bed both, not one or the other."

"Well, you and I can still trick once in a while. It doesn't have to get Wagnerian."

"Look Larry, I'll level with you: you wanted us to pretend to be lovers and actually be just tricks, fuck-buddies. And I don't want to pretend anything."

"Oh, you really think you're going to meet Mr. Perfecto and settle down for life?"

"Life, a year, ten days. Whatever, just so it's real. I'm bored with tricking and I'm off pretty, sentimental games, and they'll just start up again if we get back together."

"Frank, I have just one question: are all the other butch wop faggots as dumb as you are?"

"You can tell me when you've spread for the rest of us, which at your rate of tricking means I should hear from you in about two weeks."

Frank hung up the phone and addressed himself in a nearby mirror. "Never, never talk seriously with a silly twit. Never, never, never." Then he turned and opened the little file box on the table by the phone, fished out the card with Larry's name on it, tore it in half and let it fall to the wastebasket. He shrugged, then went downstairs to see if the mail had come.

Golden Gate Park had been a lot of fun until the fog rolled in from the Pacific, and the day had turned dull and moist. On the tedious bus ride back to their home Billy noticed that Harold seemed preoccupied and felt that something was a little bit wrong.

Back in their apartment Billy worked in the kitchen, it being his turn to cook dinner. When he had a few minutes free he leaned out of the door to talk with Harold, who sat in the living room reading a newspaper.

"Hal?"

"Yeah?"

"Uh, is anything wrong?"

Harold lowered the paper. "Not really."

"I wish that you would say what it is, especially if it involves me."

Harold's grave look gave way to a big, slow grin. "Everything in my life involves you," he said.

"So, what's wrong?"

"Well, it's just that last night, at that guy's place, you were so

24

dazzled by it all . . . I can never get anything like that for you."

"But Hal, it was a visit to a dream. That's all. I don't want to live like that."

"And I don't like it too much the way whatsisname got you off into a corner."

"Showing me his garden?" Billy asked. "He didn't try anything, and when I said I had to get back to you, he showed me right inside . . . and if you're jealous, I love it."

"I guess I was, a little," Harold said. "All gone now. I guess men will always be looking at you, wanting to get to know you better. You're pretty cute, you know."

"Not too bad yourself. Well, I think dinner is about to be served. Milk with your hamburger or a beer?"

"Milk," Harold answered. He shifted to one side of the couch when Billy brought in the heavily laden tray and set it on the coffee table.

Billy sat down beside him, and they began their meal. As Billy ate he couldn't help but feel that the room looked kind of drab and tacky, that the furniture, though decent stuff, had no real flair or distinction. There was not even a little of the magic here that in Jameson's place was everywhere. Billy thought he could improve the place bit by bit, especially after he got a part time job and had come money of his own to spend. Or maybe they could move, eventually, into some bigger, sunnier flat. He knew that Hal might not want to move, though: Hal didn't notice his surroundings much, and he was a creature of habit. Which was okay, except that it extended to bed, and sometimes Billy found himself wishing that Hal would show more interest in experiment and exploration. Their sex life was getting to be all the same, he felt; would it be like this from now on? And how could he say anything without severely hurting Hal's feelings?

"How's your burger?" Billy asked.

"Fine," Harold answered. "Salad was good, too."

Exactly what he always says when I cook, Billy thought. I wonder if he really means it.

3

On the beautiful, sunny late June morning Billy and Harold stood on the sidewalk on Market Street among thousands of other people, watching the Gay Freedom Day parade. As the various groups marched by, interspersed with bands and floats, the couple sometimes was shocked, but by and large they felt proud and happy.

"What's that?" Billy asked his taller friend. "Way down there, back of the baton twirlers. Can you tell?"

"Some kind of tower or something, on a float I guess."

In a short time a flatbed truck moved slowly into view. The tower turned out to be a lighthouse that stood among painted cardboard rocks and a tinsel ocean. A banner on the side of the truck read, in huge red capital letters,

BEACON BAR — California Street

Men dressed as sailors lounged about the paper rocks, along with a beautiful young blonde mermaid.

"Frank! Frank! Hi!" Billy yelled. He and Harold waved at their favorite bartender.

26

Trying to look at ease as he braced himself against the shivering "lighthouse" on the wobbly float, Frank smiled down at the couple and waved back.

After the truck passed by Billy said, "Someone we know. Kind of a kick, isn't it?"

Harold agreed, and a few moments later he saw another familiar face, that of Jeffrey, the young friend of Deek Jameson. He had slipped in among the crowd to reach them.

Jeffrey greeted them with bland pleasantness, then said, "My friend Deek is up there" — he pointed to a second story window a short distance up Market Street — "and he'd like you to come up and watch the rest of the parade."

"Oh, let's," Billy said to Harold, who shrugged.

They followed Jeffrey out of the crowd and up the sidewalk to a door beside a clothing store. It opened onto a long flight of stairs, which took them to a larger room on the second floor. It was bare of furniture except for a long table laden with a wide variety of hors d'oeuvres, liquor and mixers.

Simply and neatly dressed in white and blue, Jameson came out of the crowd that stood at the windows. Billy noticed that he looked older in the daylight.

"Ah, here you are. Delightful. I thought I spotted you two down there. Have some champagne, or would you prefer hard liquor?"

They chose champagne, and Jameson poured them each a glass, then they walked to the windows to watch the last of the parade.

Talk filled the air during the pauses and dull stretches, and it seemed to Harold that everybody was more polite than on the night of the party. He noted too that a great many gazes of discreet admiration went to Billy. He did not see that a goodly number of guests looked him over as well.

When the parade ended Billy and Harold said their goodbyes and thanks. Taking them to the stairs, Jameson said, "Next Wednesday night I'm hosting a little reception at a night club for Arthur Charles... the famous female impersonator."

"Oh, yes!" Billy said. "He's going to be in the Forty-niner Room at the Hotel Frisco! I read something about him in one of the gay papers."

"Yes, and I want you both to come and meet him in person. It's just a little welcome back to town. He hasn't played here in four or five years, you know, and this is where he got his start."

"Well...." Billy said, then looked to Harold, whose face expressed no emotion at all, "we'd love to."

"Good. I planned this on such short notice that I'm taking the opportunity today of passing out invitations to my friends. You know how the mails are." He handed a square envelope to Harold and another to Billy.

After they left Jameson returned to the windows and watched the couple as they appeared below on Market street, then disappeared into the immense crowd that was heading for the plaza in front of City Hall. He stood gazing at the thousands of men and knew that many of them were nice-looking, some handsome, and a goodly number beautiful — all unlike himself. He had never been anything but plain. Jameson found it ironic that age had improved his looks, not lessened them — a few character lines had helped a lot. They had developed during the lonely years of his youth, when he had concentrated on making his small inheritance into a large fortune; he had then confined his social life to brief contacts with hustlers.

Looking back, Jameson knew he had been afraid to look for love, sure he would be rejected by anyone he approached. He had toughened over the years, and his money and a certain amount of influence were shields. He could buy what he wanted now, which was good times and love — or at least a reasonable facsimile of love, the kind that can be bought. If he could not have a man who truly loved him, Jameson had the next best, men of great physical beauty and sexual versatility, preferably also socially presentable and not likely to run off with the family silver.

Jameson liked to think that love was an illusion for everyone everywhere, and he propped up this belief with the knowledge that almost everyone could be bought. On occasion, though, he was forced to admit that love did exist. The sight of lovers who lived only for each other gave Jameson a pang deep within, where all the hurts of his younger days were hidden away. He felt that what existed between lovers was something he could never experience. He knew too that, often enough, it was something very fragile.

Billy and Harold of course fascinated Deek Jameson, especially Billy, so beautiful, young, natural, and intense. That was exactly the kind of young man Jameson wanted in his life, one after another....

He turned away from the window, put on a smile, and rejoined his dwindling crowd of guests.

It wasn't until early evening that Billy and Harold returned home.

They'd spent the afternoon in the crowd at the plaza, listening to speeches, visiting the many booths put up by gay organizations, and eating a wide variety of fast foods. Afterwards they'd had a few drinks at the Beacon.

Billy showered first and then got into bed to read the Sunday paper. Harold soon joined him, hair still faintly damp. It wasn't long before the newspaper sections cascaded to the rug. After a long time, when both had become very hot, Harold breathed the usual command into Billy's ear: "Turn over, lie on your belly."

"No. This time you turn over."

"What?" Harold asked, surprised.

"Come on, Hal, let me do it to you."

Harold did not want Billy to mount him, but he could think of no good reason to refuse.

"Hal, we're lovers. We can try all kinds of things together, nothing to be ashamed of... Come on... please?"

Harold lay back, loosening his arms from Billy's body. "I really — it's — Billy, I can't."

"I get it. If you fuck me it's fine, but if you get fucked, then that makes you a faggot. Of course we do a lot of sixty-nine, and we spent all day with thousands of our brother fags, queers, fairies, pan—"

"Stop it!" Harold yelled. He had never heard Billy talk in such a sarcastic, painful way before.

They were silent for some time. Physical love was no longer the most important thing.

Finally Billy spoke: "There's just one question that I would really like to know."

"What?"

"When you're doing it to me, do you pretend that you're with a woman?"

"Never," Harold answered.

"That's something—"

"Billy, I don't know what it is, but I can't go for that, let you do that. Maybe I can get around to it, but... right now I just can't."

Gently Billy said, "Come on, Hal, don't look sad. It's no problem, really. Let's just go to sleep now and have sex in the morning."

Harold agreed, and they pulled back the covers and settled down for the night.

Billy lay thinking that if Harold would just let go, would just relax and let things happen as they would, then together they could explore fully the fascinating world of sex....

The next Wednesday evening a carefully dressed Billy stepped off a bus in North Beach. He looked around the unimpressive neighborhood for a night club, then spotted a glittering doorway over which a huge fin of a sign held aloft the name *Soldi's* in blazing red neon script. Billy crossed the street and entered the building. There he was confronted with a large sign that said *PRIVATE PARTY TONIGHT.*

A man in black came forward, looked at Billy's invitation, and nodded him through a doorway.

He walked into the huge half-circle of a theater-like room full of tables and chairs.

"Ah, my dear Billy. So good you could come. And where is Harold?"

"He had to work overtime," Billy answered, lying in order to be polite. "I'm afraid he can't come at all."

"Pity. Come with me and we'll get champagne and then meet Arthur Charles."

The famous female impersonator turned out to be an ordinary looking, masculine man who appeared neither young nor old. He was wearing a dark Brooks Brothers suit.

Billy feared he might be snubbed, feeling he was a nobody in this well-dressed crowd, but Arthur Charles greeted him with warmth and charm, and Billy, at Jameson's side, found himself to be part of the crowd gathered around the celebrity.

"What was I saying?" Arthur Charles asked nobody in particular. "Oh yes, well she was a marvelous actor, but in her early days had this addiction to entrances... the entrances of cheap hotels... No, not really. I should say she loved to *make* entrances, not work them. Well, except maybe a little, in her early years, and in her later years, and possibly in her middle years — but that's another story. This particular night she went to Goldie's, a place in midtown that was all the rage at the time. Very much the theater crowd, helpful to be seen there, meet a producer, that sort of thing. *And* Goldie's design was perfect for making entrances. You pushed through two large and heavy swinging doors, all padded in white leather, and there you were, at the top of a staircase that led down to the room itself. Well, one night she put on her newest tuxedo, hailed a taxi, and since the driver must have been quite plain and old, arived at Goldie's without a hair out of place. Well, my dears, she just pushed those doors aside, strode in and, as everybody did, came to a stop and gazed about. Just in case anyone wanted a good look? Yes, and as she stood playing her profile for all it was worth, and she *was* a gorgeous man, well, my dears, those two huge doors came swinging back again and knocked her ass over teacups down the stairs."

Billy joined in the general burst of laughter. Jameson leaned over and whispered in his ear that Arthur Charles had been talking about a certain movie star, whom Billy had seen in old movies on TV, and always in super-macho roles, often as a cowboy.

Charles went on: "Well, she made such a fuss that the management had to do something. I don't recall if they took her into the alley and beat her to a pulp or if they took her into the kitchen and gave her a warm busboy to eat."

Deek Jameson spoke as the laughter died down. "Arthur, will you tell us about Vita Dare's teeth?"

"Oh, I *couldn't*. It's much too dirty for the West Coast. And how can I tell such a vile anecdote when this blond *child* is standing here, all blue-eyed and dewy?"

Billy began to redden. All evening so far he had felt poised and almost relaxed. But now... perhaps it would be best to excuse himself and leave.

Deek Jameson put his arm around Billy and gave him a hug. "Arthur, darling, you've made him blush."

"Have I? You must forgive me, dear child. I always like beautiful men to be as relaxed as possible when they're... with me." Charles batted his eyes at Billy in such a comic manner that Billy couldn't help but relax and smile.

"Relaxed?" asked one of the men gathered around Arthur Charles. "Is that your way of saying naked?"

"No, dear, it's my way of saying lunch. Now, about this awful story I'm possibly not going to tell. Billy, are you a virgin?"

"No."

"And you're not of the straight perversion?"

"No, not at all."

"Good. I'll tell the story, and maybe I'll wring another of those divine blushes out of you. It's so rare to find modesty in San Francisco. My boy, you're an endangered species, which is always a good audience... Well, once upon a time, many years ago, in a far away land called Hollywood, there lived two very big movie stars. One of them was Vita Dare, a glamorous blond who retired when sound came in because of an unshakeable Brooklyn accent. The other was Norma Leeds, whose career petered out in the 'forties. At the time she was married to Mario somebody, and he had been the husband of Vita Dare a few years before, until her career began to slip. Mario and

Norma and Vita found themselves having a smart weekend at Marion Davies' beach house. It was expected by all that holy hell would break loose. But the two ladies were exquisitely polite to each other... so disappointing.

"Vita, however, desired to talk with Mario alone. She had some unresolved feelings about him, apparently. He wouldn't come near her. So, one night while Norma and Mario were doing whatever it is married couples do when they're still talking to each other, Vita crawled with the greatest stealth into the bedroom. She knew that Mario always insisted on one thing in bed, and she was aware that Norma owned one of the most beautiful and expensive sets of choppers ever seen in Hollywood.

"Vita's guess was right. The false teeth were sitting on the Louis Quatorze night table. Vita seized them and slipped away into the night.

"The next day Norma reported that she was feeling a little ill and would not be down for breakfast. That's when Vita's compassionate nature came to the fore: she traded the teeth for a night with Mario.

"Norma didn't care for this at all, but she had no choice. I'm sure any number of the male guests offered to keep her company through the lonely night. Perhaps one of them did. Who knows? It all happened so long ago, in the early 'thirties. It's likely that everyone who was at that weekend party is dead now.

"But I'm being morbid. Let me cheer you up with the news that I've added sereral new females to my act."

"Who? Who?" was the query, coming from every direction.

"'Enter chorus of gay owls, hooting.' Well, one is a very very big singing star with a large nose, and the other is a very very big singing star with a large behind." Charles then looked over his shoulder down toward his thin backside and said, "Acting. It's going to take acting!"

Billy stood enchanted and charmed. He had found Arthur Charles very funny, and he had been impressed at how the man had made the rather unpleasant Vita Dare story suddenly touching at the end. He wished Harold had come along, but he had arrived home tired, in a poor mood, and Billy knew he had made a mistake in trying to rush him into getting ready.

"What's so great about seeing a man who makes jokes while wearing dresses?" Harold had asked.

"Hal, you don't understand. Arthur Charles is world-famous, and it's in a night club. It'll be interesting."

32

"'Interesting,' Harold said. "Phoney baloney and more of that food that gives me a bad stomach. I'm not going."

"Hal, don't be like that."

"You go. Have a good time."

Round and round they went until Billy left by himself and caught the bus that would take him to North Beach. He felt guilty during the ride but resentful too, thinking that Harold could be a little more considerate.

His unhappy feelings had faded long since, and he chatted and sipped champagne happily, thankful to have been invited.

At the same time, a few miles away, Harold sat drinking in the Beacon.

Frank was surprised to see him alone, here for two hours now, and drinking one beer after another. He knew Harold as a very slow, light drinker. Maybe something was up. Could be that Warren was going to win the bet, and that at least would mean that Harold would be up for grabs. Feeling that Harold preferred to drink and think his own thoughts, Frank had not tried to make conversation with him all evening. Now, though, with the bar quiet and Harold full of alcohol, Frank sensed the big guy wanted to talk. He cleaned some glasses off the bar near Harold.

"Busy tonight, wasn't it?" Harold asked.

"Yeah, very, for a Wednesday."

"Warren didn't come in?"

"Not tonight," Frank answered.

"Not that I know him, but I get so used to seeing him sitting 'round at the back corner of the bar."

"Yeah, a real regular. Nice guy. Lives around here."

"Say, maybe you can tell me something, Frank. Who is Arthur Charles?"

This guy really *is* just out of the boons, Frank thought. "He's a drag entertainer, and really good. Uncanny sometimes, when he does his imitation. Up there with, like, Charles Pierce and K.T. Stevens."

"He's good? Doing imitations in dresses?"

"Well, look: It's a very ancient art form, entertainment, whatever you want to call it."

Harold emitted what sounded to Frank like a growl. The bartender realized that a guy who worked in a foundry all day and who was new to the gay world could hardly be expected to appreciate the finer points of drag entertainers.

33

"To tell the truth, Frank, Billy and I were invited to some kind of reception in a night club for this Arthur Charles guy, given by Deek Jameson. 'Deek', what a sillyass name—"

"Oh?"

"Billy wanted to go. I didn't, so he went and now I feel kind of bad about it all."

"Mmm," Frank said. He realized that Harold was anything but free of Billy. There was no use coming on with the guy tonight. Frank thought Harold was a little foolish, though, for ever letting Billy out of his sight.

Over in North Beach, at the night club, a three-piece band had shown up and was playing dance music. Billy, worried about his inability to dance with men, filled a plate with food from the buffet and found an unoccupied table far from the dance floor. Deek Jameson and Arthur Charles joined him just as he finished eating.

"To Billy," Charles said, raising his glass of champagne. Jameson followed suit.

After the toast, Arthur Charles said, "Billy, I do hope you don't hate me for teasing you. It was only meant in fun."

"I took it that way," Billy said and backed up his speech with a smile.

"Have you known Deek for a long time?"

"Well, not really."

"You two are not...?"

"No," Jameson said, "and more's the pity. Billy's lover is quiet, huge, handsome, muscular, and I can't offer much in the way of competition, can I?"

"Deek, I really don't know. You and I have never... competed. And it's too late now. I seem to have become infected with your youth-fixation, darling."

"*I* infected *you*?" Jameson asked.

"But my dear, I didn't know young men existed until I went to one of your parties and found *all of them* there.... Billy, pay no attention, we're just two battered old queens flapping our lined lips at each other."

"I like it. You're both a lot of fun."

"Why thank you, Billy," Arthur Charles said, beaming. "Of course we are, it's what I always say, and I'll show you just how much. Let's dance, Billy."

"Well, I—"

"Come on. Make an old man happy."

34

Billy quickly learned that dancing with a man wasn't hard at all, especially when Mr. Charles let Billy do the leading. Deek Jameson was Billy's second partner.

Afterwards other men asked Billy to dance, and he had fun, wishing only that they wouldn't try to dance so close.

Finally he asked the time of a waiter, and learning that it was after midnight, he felt a stab of panic. Hal must not get the wrong idea. Billy hoped his lover was in bed asleep.

Billy found Jameson to say good night, and Deek walked him to the foyer entrance. When they were alone the older man said, "My friend Quentin Wales is having a weekend yachting party, and I would like you to come. We sail on Saturday morning around ten, have brunch out on the bay, and return after dinner in the evening. Do say you'll come."

"I'd love to, Deek, but I couldn't without Harold."

"Of course not. I certainly include Harold in the invitation. I thought you understood. Here's my card with my home number. Call me if you can't come. Otherwise, it's slip 5624 at the marina, ten o'clock."

Billy said he thought they'd come, made his thank-yous for the evening, and put his hand on the panic bar of the club's front door. Jameson said "Goodnight" quite softly and let his hand pass across the fly of Billy's slacks.

Out in the street the air was cold, and a fog horn sounded somewhere to the north. Billy waited at the bus stop, eager to get home as soon as possible. He thought that Jameson shouldn't have groped him like that, but Deek had drunk a lot of champagne. Anyway, no real harm was done. It didn't mean anything.

4

On Saturday morning Billy stood beside the bed looking down on Harold, still asleep. He liked the peaceful, almost boyish look on his lover's face, contrasting with the blue shade of beard about his jaws and chin and the ferocious mat of hair that began a little below his neck. How beautiful Hal will look today, Billy thought, dressed in white slacks and blue shirt, out there on the bay.

"Harold...? Harold, wake up!"

"Mmph? What time?"

"It's eight. We have to be there at ten, and the bus takes almost half an hour."

Harold groaned and turned over. "Tired...."

"Hal, come on. You said you wanted to go."

Harold suddenly erupted from the bed, kicking the blankets aside as he sat up. He groaned, then said one word: "Coffee."

"I've made some," Billy answered and went off to the kitchen. He prepared the brew with sugar and cream, just the way Harold liked it, then carried it into the living room where Hal, now wearing his bathrobe, sat slumped on the couch.

Returning with another cup steaming in his hand, Billy sat down beside Harold. "I know you worked all week and like to sleep in on Saturday, but—"

"But that Jameson and his yachting party are more important than anything else."

"Hal, it'll be a good time."

"Sure... watching him breathing hard every time he sees you. He's after you, Billy."

"Well, maybe he is, a little, But I don't have any interest in him at all."

"You're just using him, then."

Billy knew that Harold was still annoyed because he'd come home so late on Wednesday. He'd found Hal sitting up in the living room, drunk and silent. Billy felt he should try his hardest now to keep Harold from getting in an even worse frame of mind. "Deek is inviting us maybe for one reason, and we're going for another. So what? He'll have a nice time entertaining, and we'll have a nice time being guests, and that's that."

Harold made a sound that sounded more like a groan than like any known language.

Billy thought a retreat was the best idea. He stood up and took off his robe as he said, "I better shower" and left the room.

Watching the nude figure depart, Harold was struck by a sudden mental picture, of Jameson pawing a naked Billy. Something sour bit the back of his throat, and the coffee turned to gall in his stomach. Harold wanted to curse, to break something.

When Billy returned he was fully dressed. He found Harold sitting in the same place. "You want to shower?"

"We're not going" was Harold's reply.

"But I accepted the invitation. They're expecting us."

Eyes down, half-growling as he talked, Harold said, "You just say yes every time for us both, without thinking about how I feel, and I'm tired of it."

Billy was surprised. "I didn't mean to do anything you don't like, but I thought this would be fun."

"We're different people, Billy. We're not always going to like the same things."

"Like sailing around the bay on a gorgeous day like this, in a big yacht?"

"Stuck on a boat with a lot of smooth phonies and feeling like a fool all day? Watching that Jameson character always looking at you? That's fun?"

"Hal, you don't need to feel threatened. They're nice people."

"I don't feel threatened, goddamit! I worked overtime all week, and you haven't worked at all!"

"But Hal, you know I've been trying to find a—"

"Haven't even done the laundry!" With that Harold went into the bedroom and slammed the door.

Stunned, Billy sat down slowly in a chair. He wondered what to do. Harold would want at least two more hours sleep, so it would be necessary to telephone Jameson. But it was no doubt too late to reach him at home. Billy hated the idea of taking a bus over to the marina just to make excuses. He would feel silly, and Jameson would say kind things.

Billy felt a small spurt of anger: He never swore at me before, he thought. Just because he can't stand for anybody to make a decision except him. I'm not a child. Lands me in this embarrassing situation, ruins the day. . . . What a stick-in-the-mud he is, doesn't want to go anywhere, do anything, never see any bar but the Beacon — why have we come to San Francisco if we're just going to live the same boxed-in life that we had to live back home?

Around noon Harold woke up again. He sat up in bed as the morning's argument returned to mind, making him more and more unhappy. Harold felt he had been much too nasty to Billy and wanted to make it up, to talk it out with his lover. But when he went into the living room he found a note on the coffee table:

> Dear Hal—
>   Have gone to the boat ride, will be back tonight. I am sorry we had a fight this morning. Maybe we can discuss it tonight over a few beers at the Beacon???
>
> Love, Billy

Harold felt terrible. Billy shouldn't have gone without him, but he knew his own display of foul temper had driven his lover out of the apartment. The idea that Billy may have been hurt was uppermost in Harold's mind now, nothing else. He sat for a long time, feeling very bad.

His eyes discovered a big cloth sack full of dirty clothes, leaning expectantly in the doorway, and Harold thought of something to serve as both a distraction from his unhappy mood and a means of making peace with Billy.

At the laundromat Harold filled two washers and set them churning, then sat on a bench in the warm, busy room and stared into space, oblivious to anything but his own thoughts.

"Hey, Harold!"

It was Frank, just across the aisle, stuffing clothes into a washer.

Chatting with Frank was a welcome relief from his solitude, though he said nothing about his scene with Billy. As they stood at opposite ends of a long table and folded clothes, Frank said, "I'm going up to the club for a swim. You and Billy want to come along, get in as my guests?"

"Swimming? Well, I'd really like a good swim, but Billy's not around right now. . . ."

"He can trust you with me," Frank said. "Let's dump our clothes at home, you pick up a swim suit and a towel, and we can meet and go to the club. You know, I just live two buildings up California Street from you."

Harold's first thought was to say no, to go home and punish himself by enduring the empty apartment all afternoon. . . and into the evening. ". . .will be back tonight" the note had said. Long hours away. A little company and some exercise suddenly looked very attractive.

"Well, why not?"

The athletic club was a short walk from California Street. "It's old and also straight," Frank said, "the Catholic Church's version of the YMCA, way back when. And it's not like the gay health clubs, all clones and cruising. Nothing wrong with any of that, but considering my particular job I kind of like a vacation from it all. Besides, the membership isn't too expensive."

For his part Harold felt very much at home in the athletic club, far more than he thought he would in a gay establishment, which, until Frank mentioned them, Harold hadn't known existed. The locker room reminded him of high school, long rows of lockers, narrow benches down the aisles, everything old and a little beat-up but clean and in good repair.

Harold changed into his jock-strap and swim suit without looking at anybody else in the busy locker room, not even at Frank who was changing just across the aisle.

Frank, however, was more curious. Knowing Harold was new to the gay world and its openness, he checked out his friend's body with great care, making up a complete picture from a large number of discreet glances. Frank liked what he saw; he liked it a lot, in fact.

Harold was mostly muscle and little fat, and like many big men looked better nude than dressed.

They swam, enjoyed a light lunch from the sandwich counter, observed a few games of racquetball, took another brief dip, and went to the showers.

"It's too steamy to get dry in here!" Frank yelled in the noisy, echoing shower room. "Let's go back to the lockers!"

As they stood in the aisle, swim suits flung dripping on the bench, they toweled themselves dry with vigor, and Harold no longer felt any shyness with Frank. Now they looked at each other openly and casually, as friends. Harold thought Frank's body was a pleasure to see — precisely muscled, wiry, lightly tanned, and with a nicely defined T of body hair across the chest and down the navel to the intensely black pubic hair around his dark, generous meat.

It was just before sundown, and Billy sat in a deck chair on the yacht, sipping a gin and tonic and enjoying the view. He knew it didn't take much hard liquor for him to feel giddy, so he drank with care. The day had been fine so far, starting with brunch and meeting a lot of pleasant men. And the cat-eyed Jeffrey was not present. Billy figured that young man had disappeared from Jameson's life, judging by a few vague remarks that Deek made during the day.

Soon there would be a buffet dinner and then, he was informed, dancing to taped music in the small but adequate space within and just outside the main cabin. Then the return to the marina and, for Billy, a confrontation with Harold. It was the second time this sort of problem had come up; they had to talk it out and be sure it didn't happen again. It would be so great to have Harold in the empty deck chair that stood beside his own, Billy thought. He felt he had been wrong to come on this little party alone, but he knew he couldn't let himself be ordered around by Harold, either. They were lovers, not father and son.

A thin, older man settled in the deck chair beside Billy's. It was Quentin Wales, the owner of the yacht and a close friend of Deek Jameson. His weathered face was the color of a grocery sack, with somewhat caved-in cheeks and big, rather staring, light grey eyes. "Enjoying yourself?" he asked Billy for the fourth or fifth time today.

"Very much, Mr. Wales."

"Quentin, if you will. I'm glad to hear it, and we'll all have a good deal more amusement after dark."

"Oh, the dancing, yes. That'll be fun."

"Yes. The dancing and etcetera."

Harold looked at the clock on the TV set. It was almost midnight. He had been waiting in the apartment for hours, first cleaning the place in order to keep busy, then watching television and sipping a cold beer for so long that it turned warm in his hands.

He aimed the clicker and changed to a channel with late news. Harold felt silly, but he sat through the show half afraid he might be told that a boat had sunk in the bay, had caught fire in the bay, had collided with a tanker in the bay. . . .

The newscaster said nothing of the kind. Relieved and also irritated and nervous all at once, Harold decided he could not sit and stare at the tube any longer. He wrote a quick note and headed out for the Beacon bar.

The late Saturday night crowd filled the place, but Harold found a stool at the bar all the way down at the back, next to Warren, the redhead he knew mainly by sight. They said hello, and Harold ordered a beer from the busy Frank, who gave him a big hello and a smile.

As Harold drank one beer after another, Warren could not help noticing how often he was checking the clock on the wall. And it was clear that the big guy was drinking because he was unhappy.

Behind the bar Frank worked smoothly and swiftly, and all the time thought about Harold, so sexy and sweet — a man he liked as a person, and a body he liked too. He told himself over and over that he and Harold could only be friends, but all the while his mind devised one drama after another — some probable, some pure fantasy, but all of them ending with Harold parting from Billy and becoming lovers with Frank.

At midnight on the yacht Billy didn't feel so good. Drinking, dancing, and smoking grass had followed the buffet dinner. He was sitting deep in the shadows of the stern, his head dizzy and full of sparkles and fizzes, along with a curious intensity that had fastened on his mind.

The dancing had gotten very wild, and some of the men were doing sexual things inside the main cabin. They had tried to include Billy, so he had quietly retreated to the most private place he could find. Now he sat, arms over knees, gazing out at the bay, its surface of swells and wavelets glazed and sparkling with thousands of crawling, wiggling light reflections that fascinated the young man.

I shouldn't have smoked that marijuana, Billy thought. I've never had any so strong, that made me so dizzy as I feel now. . . .

"Billy? Is that you?"

"Deek. Yes, it's me." Billy stood up, and Deek caught and steadied him.

"Are you all right? I was worried you had fallen overboard."

"I'm fine. . . just a little dizzy." As he spoke Billy felt the rich dinner stirring ominously in his stomach.

"Not seasick, are you?"

"Oh, no. Just a little woozy. . . probably the grass."

Deek sighed sympathetically. "I shouldn't be surprised. Quentin's joints contain more ingredients than an Irish stew. Well, there's a little bedroom down below, if you'd like to lie down and rest a bit."

"Er. . . that might help."

Deek led the way. "Here's the ladder," he said and preceded Billy down a narrow stairway, then led him to a small wood-paneled cabin with a bed recessed into one wall.

Billy lay down, relieved to be on a pleasantly soft mattress. His dizziness was increasing, and so were the strange lights that flashed and zoomed about in his head. From above came the sounds of fast music and the footfalls of dancers.

Sleep had come and then gone, Billy knew, because he became conscious of the noise from up on deck once more. He wondered if he had been asleep for five minutes or an hour. His time sense had glided away, the visions within his closed eyes had become sensuously entertaining, often coalescing into parts of Harold's body, and Billy, hard in his pants now, wanted most in the world to be at home in bed with Hal, having the wildest kind of sex.

As in a dream he felt his cock freed of the contraints of his clothing. Then it seemed to rise into the heat, touch, and wetness of a mouth.

Surprised at the strength of his fantasy, Billy opened his eyes and tried to focus, and when at last he could he saw that Deek's face was in his lap, that his form was half-kneelng at the side of the bunk.

"No. . . stop. Don't. . . don't do that."

Deek worked harder and harder on Billy, taking his cock far down his hot, tight throat.

Billy tried to sit up but found a coated arm could hold him down, and he lay there frightened of his great physical weakness. Gathering himself together as best he could, he struggled once again to escape, but his efforts only increased the spreading sense of pleasure in his midsection.

The ejaculation came in a riotous flood of sensation, but at the same time felt as it were happening to someone else, at some vast distance away.

At the Beacon bar the pianist was nearing the end of his last set, all Gershwin numbers. Some time earlier Harold had changed from beer to hard liquor and now was putting down the scotch almost as fast as he had drunk the beer.

Frank didn't like all this. He knew something must be very wrong, and figured that matters would improve once Billy showed up, wherever the kid had gone. Who else would Harold be getting drunk over, who else would make him brood like that? The kid better show up pretty quick, Frank thought. "Last call!" he said in a very loud, deep voice. The other bartender echoed his words.

Frank leaned close to the figure hunched over the bar and said, "Harold, stick around until I get the place closed up. We can walk home together. . . . I always feel safe on the streets with you."

The little joke brought only the hint of a smile to Harold's face, but he nodded slowly.

In a few minutes, at two in the morning, Harold accepted the cup of coffee Frank poured for him and a glass of water and some aspirins as well.

Around two-thirty Frank and Harold stepped outside the Beacon. Harold pushed off from the wall and with Frank's aid managed to get across California Street and to the entrance of his apartment building.

Once sure that Harold was safely inside, Frank started up the sidewalk to his place. It had been a long day and busy night, but Frank felt very hyper. He thought about going to the baths, then rejected the notion and knew he was going home to unwind and, ultimately, jerk off with thoughts of Harold in mind.

Billy woke to find the little cabin's several portholes glaring with sunlight. It had to be Sunday morning and he felt a jolt of panic: how would Harold react? Then Billy noticed that somebody had removed his clothes, and he was sure he'd lain down fully dressed. Then he remembered that Deek had gone down on him the night before. Billy felt lousy, and when he got up he felt even worse, his head and stomach telling him he had a severe hangover.

He dressed quickly, all the while trying to pull himself together, and went up on deck. The sunlight blazed from the cloudless sky, sparkled and shone all over the waters of the bay and glittered off every bit of metal on the yacht. It was agony for Billy to keep his eyes open for

43

more than a second or two.

When he could bear to see, he realized that the yacht was resting quietly in its slip at the marina, with the city of San Francisco gently bobbing in the distance. Nearby, on the grassy acres of Marina Green, numbers of men and women lay sunbathing while others jogged around its perimeter.

Safe, he felt.

"Ah, Billy. You're up."

Billy turned toward Deek Jameson, who was coming down the deck toward him, looking pleasant and rested, and he hated the man.

"Yeah," Billy said. "I'm up."

"I must tell you right off that I'm quite ashamed of myself. I know I took advantage. And what I did was very wrong. Perhaps Quentin's silly dope got to me too, I don't know. And certainly if I had known he was planning an out-and-out orgy I would never have invited you and Harold. Last night was just something nasty to you, I suppose, but for me, and I doubt that you'll believe this, it was an act of worship.... You must admit, Billy, that you are very beautiful. And I must tell you that I felt so bad about what I had done that I tried to make you comfortable. I even locked the door so nobody could get in. Rather ticked dear Quentin, because of course it's his cabin, but I doubt he remembers a thing. He collapsed in the midst of the revelry in the main cabin.... Well, I'm chattering. All I want is for you to forgive me."

"Sure," Billy said, all his anger drained away by the apology and by his own nausea and headache.

"I am relieved, though I can see you are not at all happy. I know you have a lover and that I'm some years older than you, Billy, but you're both so charming. So I hope that in the future we can be friends and nothing more. I just don't want last night to make us enemies."

"Mmm, guess not," Billy mumbled.

Jameson went on in an ever more kindly voice: "And I do wish your Harold would be a little more sociable. This is not to lessen the blame I put on myself for last night. But if he had come with you, none of it would have happened, would it?"

"I guess not," Billy said. He knew that the wild party of the night before would have shocked Harold completely. An orgy. With drugs. Harold would probably have dove overboard and swum for miles. He went on: "Harold, well, thinks you're after me."

"He may have been right, somewhat, I must confess. But I learned my lesson last night, Billy. From now on we'll just be friends, you and

44

I and Harold."

"Well... I better go now."

"Oh, yes. I was going to talk to you yesterday about two matters, but things got so busy — Quentin hasn't the faintest idea of how to go about being a host — that I didn't have time. The first is that the Summer Opera has a delightful opera in its repertory this season. I'm making up a party for the first night, and I very much want you and Harold to be among my guests."

"I'll have to talk to Harold about it," Billy said. It would be too rude, he thought, to refuse the invitation outright.

"Good. You'll like *Elixir of Love*. It's light, comic, full of lovely tunes, and for once the plot is quite easy to follow."

Billy gave a wan, neutral smile, nodded goodbye, and turned toward the gangplank.

"Oh, one other thing, Billy. You said something about looking for a job. Well, I do have a friend who is looking for an employee. It's a part-time position, you see, and it might be suitable for you when you begin college in the fall. My friend has a shop over in the Jackson Square area, sells fabrics, quite a chic establishment."

"Oh, well it's nice of you," Billy said, forcing himself to be polite, "but I already have something lined up."

"Let me give you a ride home," Jameson said.

"Thanks, but I'll take the bus." With that Billy walked away from Deek and off the yacht.

45

5

Billy found Harold sitting on the couch in the living room. He was un-
shaven and wearing his bathrobe. He held a white mug in his hand,
and the air was full of the odor of freshly made coffee.

"Yacht have a flat tire?" Harold asked.

"Practically. They started dancing and drinking, and the captain
passed out."

"Quite a party. You have a lot of wild sex?"

Billy loooked down at his lover, at the blank, rudely staring eyes.
"No," he answered. "I went off and hid, and wished I was back here
with you... if you want to know. You look like you were partying it
up yourself last night."

"One too many. Felt rotten about yesterday."

Harold had no more to say, so Billy went to the kitchen and got a
cup of coffee for himself. He refilled Harold's empty cup and received
a curt nod of thanks. Excusing himself to use the bathroom, Billy
found the laundry bad empty, hanging limp on its hook.

"You do the laundry?" he called out to Harold.

"Yeah."

In the living room Harold remembered the pleasant afternoon with Frank and decided to say nothing. In the kitchen, faced with nothing to do, Billy couldn't help but remember, with a lot of pain, the events of the night before. If only Hal had come along with me. If only . . . .

For the next couple of days they were polite, and each made some gesture of communication, asked for forgiveness in oblique ways, tried to understand the other. Suddenly Billy and Harold were over-whelming each other with kindness and attention. They spent a great deal of free time having sex. Their life together seemed to become a single whole again.

Harold's drinking returned to a moderate level, and Billy felt that if he had to choose between Hal or the world, Hal would easily win.

Billy's only fear was that Jameson would telephone, about the opera or whatever, and cause another uproar. After several days of edginess, Billy realized that Jameson did not know his number. The telephone was in Harold's name, which Jameson might not remember, and it was not yet in the book.

With his feeling of relief came a kind of pardon for Deek Jameson's actions on the yacht. Billy had no high opinion of them, but he realized he had not watched out for himself as much as he should have — Hal hadn't been all wrong about Jameson. But now Deek was in the past, a memory that Billy hoped would soon fade away.

It was a couple of weeks later, on a Saturday night, that Harold noticed Billy had been thoughtful for some time as they watched TV.

" Something wrong, Billy?"

"Oh, not really. I was just thinking. We were at the Beacon last night, and I guess we'll go there tonight, and . . . be nice to see some of the other places around, down on Polk Street maybe . . . just for a little change."

Harold suspected that few other gay bars would be as warm and friendly as the Beacon. It was the one public place where he felt at home in this strange city. And at the Beacon most of the regulars knew that he and Billy were a couple — and respected that fact.

"Well," Harold said, "I guess we can trot around to a few hotspots." He had had some strong lessons lately in the dangers of being stubborn. Billy had been wonderful in these last weeks, aglow with his beautiful smile.

They consulted their gay guide, made a list of possibilities in the immediate area, and started on foot down California Street. Not far from the corner of Polk Harold said, "Isn't this one of them, the Eight Ball?"

They pushed the curtain aside and went in. The bar was small and dark and had few customers. Two of them appeared to be half-asleep over their drinks. Billy and Harold sat down at the near end of the bar, far from their nodding and mumbling.

The bartender was young, thin as a whip, and wore a tight T shirt and very close-fitting blue satiny pants. His hair was as blond as Billy's, but chemistry was more responsible for the color than nature.

When he brought their beers he picked up the money from the bar, gave a lush smile, and said, "You guys look like you're new in town. I'm sure a coupla studs like you will find some action, but in case you don't, I know a place where you can get it on after two in the morning — my apartment... *love* a bod sandwich." He winked and with a rolling gait sauntered over to the cash register.

The men's room door in the back of the small room opened, and a thin young man strolled out, followed by the distinct odor of marijuana.

Billy was sure Hal didn't like one bit of this and said, "I'm ready to go any time you are."

As one they got up and headed for the heavily curtained doorway.

"Come back again when you can stay," came the mocking voice of the bartender.

Outside in the busy street Billy judged Harold to be not too upset and decided to make light of the experience. "Sort of a dump, huh?"

Harold grinned feebly and said, "What's next on your list?"

"Oh, now it's *my* list," Billy joked. "Well, how about the North Star? It's on Polk, down a ways, has an organist, and serves dinner, restaurant and bar separate. Sounds a little classier, right?"

"Only one way to find out," Harold said, pretending to be in a better mood than he was.

The two-block walk down Polk Street gave many young men the opportunity to cruise Billy or Harold or both. Harold was so preoccupied noticing the men who eyed Billy that he didn't see those who were eyeing him. And he did not see that Billy ignored them all.

The North Star was on a corner, a large bar with several levels and a restaurant hidden off to one side. An electric organ occupied most of a huge niche in one corner, and a handsome but pudgy man of indeterminate age was playing a wildly exaggerated version of music from *A Chorus Line*. The room was packed.

With a good deal of twisting and squeezing, Harold and Billy found some relatively clear space in which they could stand and listen to the music. Or so they thought. Some mysterious hand groped Harold fore and aft, he jumped in surprise and knocked over a passing cocktail waiter with a heavily laden tray.

The noise brought the organist to a stop. "Well, *really!*" he said.

"Sir, I'm going to have to ask you to leave," a white-shirted man said to Harold.

"Somebody goosed me," he replied, furious. Several men nearby giggled.

"Sir, we feel you should leave."

Scowling, Harold ploughed his way through the crowd with Billy following in his wake.

Outside Billy said, "Boy, are they confused. Come on, Hal, don't take it all that seriously."

"I've never been thrown out of anywhere, and some stupid — never mind."

"Well, you are sexy, and some creep wanted to know you better, and the rest of it just happened... one of those dumb things where nobody knows what's really going on...."

"I guess you're right, Billy."

"Maybe they were a little scared you'd break a few necks or something.... Well, let's try someplace else, some nice quiet, not very crowded, classy joint."

"Nah. That's enough for tonight. We're going home."

Billy hated the way Harold said what they were going to do. He had little interest in continuing alone, but he was determined, as he thought he had made clear to his lover, not to be ordered around.

"You may be going home, but I want another beer or two. It's early."

Harold thought Billy had no consideration for bruised feelings. "I think it's time for both of us to go home. We can have a nightcap at the Beacon." Harold didn't want even that, but it was better than getting Billy upset any more than he already was.

"The Beacon? We're over here on Polk Street. And I don't think it's time for us both to go home. I'm going down the street to the Wild Mare. If you're coming, fine; if not, I'll see you back at the apartment."

Finished speaking, Billy walked on down the sidewalk, hoping Harold would fall in step beside him, knowing they could relax over a beer together somewhere, maybe even laugh at their misadventures of earlier in the evening.

At the corner, where he had to wait for a light to change, Billy looked back. Harold was nowhere in sight. "Gone home," he said to himself. He crossed the street automatically, swept by sadness. He was no longer interested in exploring the gay bars around Polk Street, but he felt he could not go right back home. Why did Hal always have to be so suspicious about life, so negative, so contented with simple, boring routine? What was wrong with having a little fun? And that tacky bar and that incident at the North Star, were they such terrible events? They were small matters, trivial. He had to make Harold understand one thing: Hal was not his ruler. Hal had to treat him as an adult, let him stand on his own two feet.

Billy decided to stay out until the bars closed. That meant he'd have to drink a few drinks and a lot of club sodas. He had no choice.

Checking down the list in his hand, Billy picked another drinking place.

Harold lay on the bed gazing at the TV set and comprehending very little of the late movie. He wore only boxer shorts and a pair of socks. The other clothes lay all over the floor. On arriving home after parting with Billy, Harold had begun drinking bourbon and water. Then he switched to just bourbon, which he'd been downing now for several hours — it almost had all the pain neutralized.

The apartment entry door opened and shut. Hearing this, Harold looked at the clock on the night table; it was one-thirty in the morning.

He lay still, listening for the familiar footsteps and thinking he and Billy had to settle all this. He had known of too many straight marriages that were mutual torture setups, and he didn't want anything like that with Billy, Keep it calm, keep it peaceful, he told himself.

Billy filled the doorway, lit from behind by the weak light in the hallway. Once again Harold was jolted by his lover's beauty, his boyishly tentative way of moving, his unsure smile. Sitting up straighter against the pillow to hide the fact that he was getting hard in his unbuttoned shorts, Harold asked gently, "Have a good time?"

"It was okay. I saw about five bars. Two were kind of nice, places we might enjoy." Billy came into the bedroom as he spoke and began to undress. He noticed sadly that Harold had had a lot more than his usual few drinks, that he had thrown his clothes all over, which he usually didn't do, and that he lay on top of the bed like a slob, in his socks and the underwear with the gaping fly.

Billy hoped that Harold's quiet question meant there'd be no big scene tonight. He'd been rehearsing a carefully phrased speech about being allowed to grow up, about being trusted, about the dangers of ruts and routines, about how much he loved Hal and hated to hurt him.

Harold gazed at Billy as the blond became naked and thought of the fancy parties and rides on yachts his beauty would bring him, all the things Harold knew he could never give.

"You saw five bars?" Harold asked.

"Yeah."

"And all those guys saw you." With that Harold rose from the bed and went to Billy, standing at the dresser. His impulse to hold, to keep, to possess was overwhelming.

"Hal, come on," Billy said. He twisted free of the familiar arms, which held him captive for only a moment before they fell away. Hal's smell, which he knew so well and loved, was fouled by the sweet, cool reek of bourbon.

"Billy, come here."

To Billy's ears the voice was slurred and commanding, and he hated the sound, hated Harold to be like this.

Harold took a few unsteady but swift steps and engulfed Billy in his arms. "I want you so much, I want you with me, I wish you were ugly so everybody out there wouldn't want you, I—"

"Hal, let me go."

"Billy, don't be like that. I want you now, forever. I want you so much."

As Harold spoke he bore his lover down to the bed. Billy resisted with all his strength, trying to escape but unable to bring himself to attack Harold. Soon he lay face down under the much greater weight of Harold's body, pinned motionless in the grip of two powerfully muscular arms.

"Hal! Don't!"

Billy kept on yelling, even as he felt himself being entered, dry and without lubricant. In his pain and anger Billy briefly flashed on the idea of relaxing and cooperating, but he was too outraged, too furious to do anything but resist, to keep his muscles rigid and to hope that Hal would have an unguarded moment that would allow escape.

The pain became agony as Harold forced himself inside.

Harold felt the charge building deep in his haunches, but his mind kept running to other matters, to stabs of anxiety, and a fear of loss. Determined to possess Billy completely, he pumped on and on, harder

51

and harder. All the while he pawed the man in his embrace, pressing him closer to himself.

At last he came, shooting in deep, prolonged thrusts.

The moment Harold relaxed, Billy slid from the bed, fell to the floor, and disappeared into the bathroom.

Boozily, Harold observed the ceiling and wondered how he could have done such a thing, he who prided himself on never misusing his strength, and in the next thought it was Billy's fault, for driving him to drink — the kid was reaping what he had sown, and now maybe he would understand... understand....

In a while Billy came back into the bedroom. He found Harold asleep, sprawled over the jumbled mass of bedclothes, and smelling of cooled sweat and bourbon. Feeling the tears coming, he fought them back and turned away.

Dressing quickly and silently, noting some twinges of pain from strained muscles and patches of raw skin, Billy left the apartment. Outside, he knew, the summer fog had rolled in and made the night cold. And it was late. But Billy knew he could not stay here tonight.

Harold was late to work the next morning, and once there he felt both sick and frantic. He called home every chance he had, hoping to hear Billy's voice. Nobody answered.

He rushed back to his apartment after work. Stepping inside, Harold heard sound in the bedroom. There he found Billy packing his suitcase.

"Billy."

"Hello, Harold."

"Last night, Billy... What I did was all wrong, I know that. It was just that—"

"I'm sure you have a fine excuse, but it just doesn't matter now."

"Billy, you can't just leave."

"Yes I can. And if you want to get physical with me, I'll raise so much hell that somebody will call the police and you'll get thrown out of here."

"Billy!"

"I didn't yell last night because I thought I loved you... but I've had some time to think." He closed his suitcase.

"Please stay, Billy. Please. Anything you want, and I'll never—"

"Hal, inside my head I left you last night, while you were raping me."

"Raping you? I was too rough, maybe, but—"

52

"Too rough is exactly what you were, a whole lot too rough. I won't be treated that way."

Suitcase in hand, Billy went to the bedroom doorway. He stopped and said, "I took twenty dollars. I'll send it back as soon as I get my first paycheck."

Harold stood unmoving, astounded, and horrified. Pain seemed to take over and freeze his body. When he could move he took a few reeling steps out of the bedroom. He saw Billy going out the apartment door, coat in one hand, suitcase in the other.

"Billy!" he called out, but his knotted throat produced no more than a harsh whisper which was drowned out by the sound of a door closing.

The next day Billy left his Tenderloin district hotel and went job hunting. He had been doing a lot of thinking in his small, ugly, not particularly clean room, thinking and reading want-ads in the newspapers. All of them, it seemed, required that applicants be experienced.

That morning he applied for two jobs. One had been filled, and his part-time work background was not sufficient for him to be considered for the other.

That afternoon he registered at the state employment office, where for lack of specific skills he was classified as laborer. Then he was told to find a job listing on the laborer bulletin board. The openings were few and located far away. He couldn't see himself picking fruit in the Central Valley — he wasn't even sure where the Central Valley was. Billy left the employment office in dejection. He thought he should apply for unemployment benefits, but his pride would not let him do that.

The next morning, pride somewhat wilted and money almost gone, Billy found a pay phone.

"Mr. Jameson? Uh, yes it's Billy. I . . . I'm calling about that job you mentioned? I . . . I'm on my own now, and I need to get something pretty soon."

Billy waited through what seemed to him a long period of silence, half expecting to hear some sarcastic remarks or merely the noise of a phone being hung up.

"Oh, I see," the voice said quietly and continued in a gentle manner: "Well, come up for lunch, and we'll talk about it. I do believe Corin would find you an excellent employee. About one p.m., here at my place?"

"Well, fine," Billy said, as relieved as if he had already gotten a job.

The luncheon table, beautifully set, was located next to one of the huge windows in the apartment; the city thus made a beautiful background for Billy and Deek's conversation.

Billy said nothing about the reasons for his break with Harold, only that it had happened. He appreciated the fact that Deek Jameson was very understanding and sympathetic without being too inquisitive.

At the end of the meal, as they were having coffee, Deek said, "Billy, let me ask you a rather personal question."

"Okay."

"Do you like me?"

"Yes, I do."

"Despite the events on the yacht?"

"Sure. That was partly my fault, anyway."

Jameson smiled. "Not really, but it's generous of you to say so. Billy, I'm fond of you, and I have been since we met. I haven't felt like this for anybody in a long time, but the liking I have for you is, well, extraordinary."

"Well, thank you," Billy said. He kept smiling, but he was pretty sure this was a lead-in to a proposition, and his mood was low. Billy wondered if he would let Jameson have him if that was the only way to get a job, and he comforted himself with the thought that Jameson, if older, was nice enough, and at least he was somebody Billy knew. It wouldn't be exactly the same as whoring, he thought — but still, he was pretty sure he wouldn't do it.

"I know you can't feel so intensely about me, but that doesn't matter, just so long as you can bring yourself to like me."

"Deek, that isn't hard."

"Here is my idea. Three times a week somebody comes in to handle my correspondence, the social side, not the financial. Invitations, household matters, ticket ordering, buying books and records, all that sort of thing. After your call this morning I asked myself, why pay a stranger a good salary when I could have a friend doing the same work?"

"Well, great. I mean, it sounds perfect. But it's such a surprise. What about that job with the fabrics guy?"

"I believe it's still open," Jameson said, "but the pay would be about the same and the hours a lot longer."

"Well, it's great, but so sudden. I mean, I'll have to think for a little bit. I don't mean to sound ungrateful; it's just—"

"Billy," Jameson said with great firmness as he put his hand on the younger man's, which lay still on the table cloth, "listen to me: there

54

are no strings attached. I will not be chasing you around the desk, if that's what you're worried about."

"Oh, but I wasn't—"

"After the misfortune on the yacht? Of course you were, Billy, and I don't blame you."

"It's really that, well, this is going to sound awful, but I'm worried that you're just making up a job for me, because you feel sorry for me." Billy knew he was half-lying, but it seemed a useful cover-up for his previous reluctance to take the job, a reluctance which now was all gone.

"Nonsense. You'll find it a lot of work, real work. Come, I'll prove it."

Laying his napkin aside, Billy followed Jameson through the huge apartment and into a room crowded with file cabinets and a large desk. On it sat a typewriter and a dictating machine.

"You see?" Jameson asked.

"I feel a little bit—"

"Nonsense, my boy. I understand perfectly. Can you start tomorrow?"

"I'd love to, Mr. Jameson."

"Deek, please. Always."

A while later, after Billy filled out the necessary forms for employment, and Deek had seen the young man's current address, he said, "Here's an advance on your first week's salary," and tucked a little rectangle of folded bills into Billy's shirt pocket.

Billy left Deek in a very happy state. He felt safe again.

Every night after work Harold drank in the Beacon bar, quietly reaching a certain state. Then, when he was inside the little inner room of drunkenness, where all is mercilessly clear but gives no pain, he would leave and go home, there to examine his thoughts until unconsciousness came. He saw that he had driven Billy away, into the streets and to a fate that Harold didn't want to imagine. Billy, who knew nothing of the world, who was so trusting, who thought so well of the human race.... Harold realized too that he himself didn't belong in San Francisco; he was too staid. Yet it would be useless to return to his old home town, where all his bridges had long since been burned. With woozy detachment Harold concluded that he had reduced his life to nothing.

On one of these nights, after Harold had left the Beacon, saying goodnight gravely and walking away with the stiff dignity of someone who will not allow himself to appear as drunk as he feels, Frank took ten dollars out of his pocket and passed it over the bar to Warren.

"Guess you were right," Frank said. "Looks like they've busted up."

"Wish I'd been wrong. Harold is really saucing it."

"Yeah. . . ."

"You kind of like him," Warren said.

"Kind of, but no use making moves now. He's all inside himself. Maybe, in a while, I'll try to cheer him up. Take him to the Forty-niner Room to see Arthur Charles, something like that."

"Well, between you and Arthur Charles, I'm sure he'll be cheered up . . . but Frank, it's beginning to sound like you've got the silver pattern already picked out."

"Maybe I have. So what?"

"So nothing, and no offense intended."

"None taken," Frank said, sharpness gone from his voice.

"Good," Warren answered, knowing Frank was indeed offended. "Put me down for a toaster." He saw Frank smile at that and relaxed again. Warren realized that he had been a little bothered by his friend's open interest in Harold. Why mess with all that romantic stuff, if only grief was to follow? And he knew he'd prefer Frank to do without unhappiness as much as possible; he was a good friend, after all. It did not occur to Warren, though, that when he saw evidence of the existence of something more than mere sexual attraction between men, he became irritated, faintly suspicious that he might be missing something in life, something besides painful illusions.

6

Billy found the work a little difficult, because he had to be careful of all the details, but he liked earning his own money, and Deek frequently invited him along to shows and cocktail parties, took him out to lunch on days he didn't work, and generally saved him from having to spend much time in his dreary hotel room. It was now in a better hotel in a slightly better neighborhood, but Billy didn't want to spend any more money than necessary: he never wanted to be jobless and down to his last few dollars again.

One morning while working in the office at Deek's, Billy suddenly felt a great sadness overcome him, a sense of loss. Memories of Harold came unceasingly, good ones as well as bad, and by lunchtime, at the glass table by the window, Billy sat almost silent.

To Jameson it looked like the young man was trying to converse cheerfully and failing rather badly. "I gather something's on your mind," he said to Billy.

"Oh, it's nothing," Billy said. In a short time, urged to speak and feel better for doing so, and soothed by Jameson's kindness, Billy described his last terrible night with Harold. He ended with tears of anger in his eyes.

Jameson calmed him and at the end of the day said, "There's a lovely party tonight. I'll pick you up at nine."

"Well, that'd be really nice. It's just that I'm still a little down and might not be very good company."

"Nonsense. A little diversion should be the best treatment for your case of the blues. Do say you'll come with me."

"I'd love to. I'll be ready at nine, in the lobby."

That evening Harold came into the Beacon and surprised Frank by saying, "I decided to stop all the heavy boozing, and I had a couple of drinks at home. What can I order that isn't sweet and doesn't have booze in it?"

"Well, try a club soda with a squeeze of lime," Frank said. "Nothing to it but bubbles, not even any calories."

"Give me one of them."

Harold spent several hours downing club soda from tall glasses, finished off with a beer, and went home sober. Frank was glad to see Harold trying to shape up, but he sensed the guy was still pretty unhappy. I could get him on the rebound, Frank thought, not for the first time, but that would just be a one-night stand or a one-week scene. And it's no use trying for a relationship unless it has room to develop. Yeah, and very pretty, but I really want his body too. Maybe I'm a jerk for not taking advantage of the situation. But, the other way, if it went somewhere, Harold and me, that would be so fine. I don't know, maybe I should settle for what I can get, which may be all there is. . . . He might meet somebody great tomorrow.

For the rest of the shift, as he made drinks and change, Frank thought first one way and then the other, devised schemes and discarded them, felt good about himself, then bad. He went home quite tired and fell asleep almost at once.

He dreamed of Harold.

Jameson brought several friends back to his place for a nightcap, and Billy was one of them. As the get-together was breaking up Jameson suggested Billy stay over. "It's only a few hours until you're supposed to report to work, though I will understand if you start somewhat later than usual."

"Well, if it's not inconvenient."

"Not at all. We'll have a last little drink and a bit of a talk as soon as I see my other guests off."

Billy waited in the living room, sitting on one of the couches that faced the windows, gazing thoughtfully at the view.

Deek came back with two small liqueur glasses. "Amaretto," he said, "a little sweetness after all that salty food. I don't know where Morgan finds his caterers — always grim, his buffets. Well, and you Billy? Feeling better now?" Jameson asked this while seating himself beside his guest.

"Much," Billy said. "Thanks to you." He raised his glass and toasted Jameson, then took a sip of the pleasant liquid. "You know, Deek, I like you very much. You've been really great to me."

"Well, thank you, Billy." Jameson spoke soft and low.

"Things have been a little tough, like I told you, and I didn't think anybody would really give a damn, and it was very, well, frightening for a while." Billy felt an unusual strength of emotion as he talked. "I could have called my mother to help bail me out, but it would have been a real defeat, you know? And she isn't making a lot anyway, hasn't got much to spare, and... well, I like you very very much, Deek."

"I'm glad you feel as you do, Billy, and that I could be of help. I like you a great deal, too, and sometimes I want to express my feelings more strongly than I allow myself to do. I know I am thirty-something years older and by no means a beauty, but.... Billy, this will tell you what I really feel." Jameson took Billy's hand and drew it from the young man's thigh to his own, then pressed it firmly against his crotch.

Billy felt something warm and rubbery-stiff. He closed his fingers over it and gripped it.

Jameson swung down to the carpet, eagerly kneeling in front of Billy, between his open legs. Trembling with excitement, he reached out to the fly of Billy's slacks and zipped it open.

A few nights later, Harold was sitting in his usual spot at the back of the Beacon bar drinking club soda. He was about to order his last drink, a beer, and knew that he was staying much later than usual. But the bar had little business, Frank was such a nice guy, and the apartment was so lonesome. . . .

Far up in front the door swung open with a snap and Harold looked up to see a willowy blonde woman coming in. She approached Harold down the aisle along the bar and went on past, to disappear through a door marked WOMEN.

In a short time she returned and sat down a stool away from

Harold, who noticed that her hair was no longer all messy but carefully arranged. And he saw she was very attractive, if a little heavily made up for her years. He thought the shiny black slacks fit her body a little more tightly than really necessary, but she looked good in them and in her silky white V-neck blouse.

"Hey, Baker, I didn't see you come in."

"Your back was turned, honey. Got some scotch and some rocks back there?"

"Sure." Frank started making the drink. "Something up? You're a little twitchy."

"Some drunk thought I was hooking, and he got very physical, messed up my hair and stuff. So I ran in here. Be all right in a minute."

What a tough female, Harold thought disapprovingly.

"Who's the handsome hunk?" Baker asked.

"This is Harold."

"Very pleased to meet you," Baker said, smiling warmly.

"*Were* you hooking?" Frank asked Baker.

"Me?" the blonde asked back, all innocence. "Now Frank, you know I stopped that last year, ever since I got in the show at the Forty-Niner."

"That's right. I forgot."

"All I was doing was going home. Really, you'd think you'd be safe up in this neighborhood."

"Yeah, but there've been some incidents lately," Frank said. "Coupla bashings."

Harold thought that a woman who dressed like that and who came on so strong with strangers was bound to get herself into all kinds of trouble. If she's stopped being a hooker, he thought, she should stop dressing like one. And talking so tough.

He watched Baker drain the glass of scotch.

"Well, better get home before it gets any later," Baker said, "and, Harold, if you want to come home with me, well we could have a nice cocktail... and pretty much anything else you want... no charge, of course. Frank has no doubt given you the wrong idea about me with his huge big mouth."

"Uh, thanks... but I can't."

Standing now, Baker ran a well manicured hand up and down Harold's shirt sleeve. "Pity. Big men with tons of muscle are just my type.... Ummm, nice chest."

"Baker," Frank said, "put down those shirt buttons. That all belongs to me."

"Oh. Listen, Harold, if he ever starts treatin' you bad, come see Baker. I'll take the very best care of you. Goodnight, now.... And good night, lucky Frank."

With that Baker sauntered voluptuously to the front of the Beacon and went out the door.

From time to time, Harold had had some thoughts of going back to women, but he certainly would never want to get involved with a woman like that, even if she had raised his temperature a few degrees.

"Thanks for getting her off me," Harold said.

"Service of the house. Listen, come to think of it, the show she's in is really good, this time. It's Arthur Charles.... The female impersonator? Been around for years, really hysterical. Remember, the one you asked about?"

"The guy who tells jokes while wearing a dress?"

"Ah, come on Harold, loosen up. You won't catch anything."

"Well, I know, but — Baker! She's... one of them?"

"You didn't know?" Frank asked, surprised.

"Baker is a man? Wearing women's clothes?"

"That's right."

"I need a beer."

"Coming up."

After a couple of healthy gulps Harold said, "I can't understand why any man would want to dress up in women's clothes."

"Neither do I," Frank said. "And neither does Baker. But there it is. Anyway, they're harmless."

"It's such a strange idea to get used to."

The front door opened and Baker walked in, moving fast in high heels that made quite a noise on the floor. "Frank, hate to be a bother, but I think I need that taxi after all."

The door banged again and a man came into the Beacon. He was weaving, his suit coat hung unbuttoned, and his mean, plain, fortyish face clearly showed him to be drunk. "Hey, baby! Whatsamatta? Too good to go wi't me? Fuckin' bitch, commere!"

The man had come to where Baker stood, which was right next to Harold, who was watching all this with amazement.

"Wanderin' aroun' late at night," the man went on, "I know what you want... and believe me, baby, I got it, right down here."

Harold stood up and said, "I think you better get out of here, mister."

Just as he rose, Frank vaulted the bar. "He's right, mister. Better get out of here."

After focussing carefully on one man and then the other, the intruder turned and walked out of the bar, grumbling and staggering as he went.

Frank went around behind the bar and called a taxi.

"I want to thank you both," Baker said. "You're very kind. Like to buy you guys a drink."

"Two beers, coming up," Frank said. "You want a fast one before the taxi comes?"

"How about a shot of scotch?"

As they drank, Baker looked Harold over once more, then said to Frank, "You should bring your friend to the show."

"That's just what we were talking about," Frank said.

"I'll leave some tickets at the door. What night?"

"I'm off Sunday and Monday."

"Try Sunday. We're closed Mondays."

"Taxi," said the man leaning in the door.

"Right there," Baker answered. "'night, guys... and thanks again."

After Baker had gone, Harold said, "Well, that was something different in my life.... Better get home and hit the sack."

"Right. How about Sunday evening?"

"Well, why not? I'd like to, Frank."

"Great, and I'll call you Saturday when I'm going down to the club to swim, see if you have the time."

"Oh, one question. I never saw Baker in here before. Do those types come in here?"

"Not very often. A lot of the other customers don't like drags. Same in a lot of bars. Baker's a friend, though, and everyone likes her, so.... Hey, remember the float on Gay Freedom Day?"

"Sure."

"Baker was the mermaid."

The next morning on Nob Hill, Billy and Deek sat at the table by the window, having a last cup of coffee after breakfast. "Billy?" Jameson asked, "Do you like me enough to live here with me?"

"What? Live here with you? I... do like you, Deek."

"You want a little time to think about it?"

"I— yes."

Jameson picked up his cup and saucer. "I'll be reading the paper in the living room," he said.

Billy stared out at the city and thought hard and carefully. Living here would mean he and Deek would be lovers. Jameson lived a magical existence, true, he was kind and generous and sympathetic, and certainly helpful when help was most needed. He wasn't young, strong, or handsome, but he kept his body in good shape, and he wasn't ugly. In bed he knew a lot about pleasing another man. It was comforting when Deek was protective, too — very comforting.

But it wasn't the same as it had been with Harold, Billy knew. This was everything good but nothing blazing. Would it be right, then? And what would Hal think about his living with a rich, older man?

Billy realized all of a sudden that he was thinking in terms of still being Harold's lover. And he was nobody's lover at all. Of all people, Harold should be the last man in the world to be running his life. Bitterly, Billy felt that he would never love again, would never be able to trust and love any man so completely as he had adored Harold.

He gazed out at the city, at its thousands of pale walls standing like rows of teeth and tombstones on the hills. He asked himself what he would do if he didn't live with Deek. More loneliness in his room in the hotel? Hanging out in bars alone and bored, like that night he went out and returned to a drunken Hal, who then — no, no use to think of that and get angry again. Best to think of Deek Jameson and of an answer to his question, "Do you like me enough to live here with me?"

Billy realized that Jameson had not said love, merely like. And I do like him, Billy thought.

He went into the living room. "Deek?"

Jameson looked up from his newspaper.

"I think it would be really nice to stay with you."

"You've made me very happy," Deek said.

On Sunday night Frank took Harold to the night club where the Arthur Charles Revue was playing.

Harold looked around the elegantly decorated room and as ever, began to feel nervous in the midst of a crowd that was made up mostly of gay men. He felt a little more at home when the waiter greeted Frank as a friend before he took their drink order.

A man in a tuxedo approached the small white piano at one side of the platform. As he sat down and began to play a fast song about show business, the lights dimmed. Harold felt excited, as Frank noticed out of the corner of his eye. Suddenly light blazed all over the platform, and from an entrance on one side out came a chorus line of eight or ten dancers dressed in the net stockings and brief, spangled costumes of the gay 'nineties. Harold found it hard to believe all these kicking, prancing "ladies" were men.

As they sang and danced to a medley of old popular songs, the chorus line "accidentally" lost the key and after some amusing efforts by the pianist found it again.

"That's Baker," Frank said, "third from the right."

Fascinated to recognize someone, Harold watched Baker through the end of the number.

After the appluse had died and the chorus had marched off in unison, a voice came over a loudspeaker: "And now we present the one, the only... Arthur Charles!"

There, in a sudden shaft of light, stood someone who looked to Harold like anybody's mother wearing her oldest dress. Before his wide eyes Arthur Charles became Bette Davis, Elizabeth Taylor, Jackie Kennedy, and several other famous women. Harold was amazed: Charles not only sounded perfect, his face even changed to look much like the person he was imitating.

Frank watched the show and his guest both, and he was relieved that Harold laughed without reserve at the blue jokes that Charles scattered around like birdseed.

In about half an hour the comedian bowed off to wild applause and foot pounding, leaving Frank and Harold nearly exhausted from laughing.

Charles returned almost at once to thank the audience. "You're very wonderful and special to me. I'll be back for the rest of my show in a little while, but right now you'll see some of the local girls — you saw them in the chorus line — doing what they do best, at least in public. To begin, let me say that of all the great ladies of stage and screen, there's one I've never done. I leave that to... Baker!"

The room went dark, a flourish of chords came from the piano, and a single spotlight slowly grew larger and larger. It revealed a beautiful blonde wearing black gloves and a long, sparkling, tight, red dress.

The audience gasped at the perfect illusion, then broke into applause. "Diamonds Are a Girl's Best Friend" came from the piano, and Harold sat there astounded. He had rarely seen anything so incredible. The face, the singing voice, the movements, everything was exactly right.

Other acts followed by other members of the chorus, but Harold hardly noticed them. When Arthur Charles returned he was wearing a beautiful evening gown. He imitated three top female movie stars of the forties and fifties, each battling the others to see which would end up in bed with Montgomery Clift, who was passed out upstairs.

As Harold stood up he noted that his stomach muscles ached from all the laughing he had done. That's when he saw Billy, in the crowd of people coming in for the second show. He was beautiful as ever, wearing new clothes, and his haircut looked expensive. He appeared happy, chattering with Deek Jameson at his side.

Realizing what Harold was looking at, Frank said, "We go out this way, the side door." Harold started moving and they joined the crowd leaving the night club.

Outside they decided to walk to Polk Street, which was only a few blocks off. Frank didn't know what to say, but he was sorry Harold's good mood had been spoiled, and he doubted now that he could get his friend into bed tonight. The kind of love affair you get over, he thought, but not the kind you forget. All that hassle in that nowhere town, coming out here — too bad, it really is.

"I could use a couple of drinks," Harold said.

"Sounds good to me. Any place special you want to go?"

"Where I haven't been before, a real dive, maybe."

"Well, one of the trashiest gay bars in the city is about two blocks away."

"Let's go."

The bar was not well lit but looked glittery-crummy in decor. As they sat and talked Frank quietly identified the men he figured must be hustlers and who he thought were dealing dope. After they had been there for and hour or so a fight broke out, two lean young men going at each other with pool cues. At once the two bartenders ran from behind the bar, surprisingly fast for their height and beefiness, and bum's-rushed the two young fighters out into the street. One bartender went on out the door, jerked a cue stick from the cursing man's hand, came back inside and returned it to the rack on the wall near the pool tables.

"You wanted a dive," Frank said.

"Looks like I got it," Harold answered.

Another round of drinks and Frank suggested they go. Harold agreed easily, and Frank began to hope this evening would end well. Harold had not been interested in any kind of personal talk this night, and Frank was sure his mind had been elsewhere. But now, out in the street, dark and all Sunday quiet, maybe Harold would come back to the moment and want to climb into bed with Frank.

Harold remained silent until they reached California Street, when he said, almost as if to himself, "That's what Billy is . . . like those guys."

"A bar brawler?" Frank asked, surprised.

"No, like the guy with the tattooed arms talking with the old man over in the corner, getting beers out of him."

"A hustler?"

"Yeah... a whore."

Frank heard a lot of bitterness in Harold's words. He felt the best thing he could do was keep silent.

"A kept man, a prostitute!" Harold said. "And how, I do not know, but I drove him to it. I know I did."

Frank could think of nothing to say that would help.

They walked up California in silence for several blocks.

"Well, here's where I live," Harold said. "You want to come up, have a few drinks, maybe fool around some?"

Frank said, "I'd like to, but I'm really tired. Let's keep it for a few days and you come over to my place for dinner."

"Sounds fine. Guess I kind of got depressed tonight. Really good the way you hung in there. But it hurt to see him all dolled up like that, his hair combed so fancy...."

"Take it easy," Frank said. "Remember, you can only run one life at a time, and you can't ever really know everything that's going on inside anyone else's head. Right?"

"I guess so.... Thanks, Frank. I enjoyed the evening a lot."

"Good night, Harold."

Frank went home wondering if Harold was right about his ex-lover. Maybe Billy was just blinded by the glamour and the money, maybe not. Frank thought he and Harold would have had a far more romantic evening had Billy not shown up at the night club with that Jameson character. But there would have been no point in accepting Harold's invitation to come up and have a few drinks. Harold was lonely, and Billy was still a large presence for him. Frank knew from a good deal of experience that there was no competing with a past that was still so painfully vivid. He was not, after all his trouble and waiting, going to involve himself in a three-way. Harold would have to think of Billy less, so Frank would have a chance to be noticed, have a possibility of being the center of Harold's life.

If he can't mentally let Billy go, Frank thought, then I guess Harold and I won't have a chance in the world of getting something good going. Have to settle for another one-night stand.... Shit. Why is it the men I like are always impossible to reach? Warren not believing in love, Harold hung up on Billy. Guess all I can do is keep looking, not give up....

7

"Billy, you look beautiful, just perfect," Deek said. He was standing beside a trim young man who had a measuring tape draped over his shoulders, and both of them were looking closely at Billy. He stood at the full-length mirrors in the fitting room, wearing jeans and examining the tight black leather chaps he had just put on.

The admiring young salesman helped Billy into a black leather vest, slipping it onto his bare upper body.

"Marvelous," Deek exclaimed. The salesman quietly agreed.

Turning this way and that in front of the multiple mirrors, Billy saw that the chaps sharply defined his legs and lower body. His small buns looked more prominent, and the bulge in the crotch of his jeans was accentuated. Billy felt he looked a bit exaggerated, a little strange.

"Well, Billy, what do you think?" Jameson asked.

"Looks great," Billy said. "Smells good, too." He overemphasized his enthusiasm for the outfit not so much to please Deek but as part of his policy of entering into his new life as fully as possible. He welcomed the many novel distractions that kept away the memories of his first love, both its pleasant moments and his bitterness for the way it ended. He had decided to run from the past by embracing the present. And with Jameson his life now was busy and quite different from the way it had been before.

Everything had changed the morning he said he would live with Deek. He had expected to have a room in the apartment, but Jameson showed him to a suite. Furnished in very masculine and handsome fashion, the living room opened onto a bedroom. There a huge, curtained picture window offered a spectacular view of the city. And Billy discovered he had his own small, complete bathroom.

"Wow.... Really nice, all this," Billy said, then asked, apprehensively, "But how much would my share of the rent be?"

Jameson chuckled in a kindly manner. "My boy, let me be quite vulgar for a moment: I make a great deal of money; it just pours in. Rent and groceries are concerns that you needn't worry about for a moment. Promise me you won't think twice about them. I want you to spend your salary only on your own needs and pleasures."

Rather overwhelmed, Billy agreed.

He found it strange at first to wake up around noon and have breakfast, but he soon became adjusted to these hours, because he did, after all, stay up until very late at night. Deek knew all kinds of people, so there were always cocktail parties and dinners, celebrities to meet, shows in nightclubs and visits to the city's nicer gay bars, in the upper Fillmore area.

And there was sex. For an older man Deek liked a lot of it, and he wanted Billy to be on top, which the younger man found very enjoyable. And Deek knew all kinds of things to do in bed, which Billy thought fascinating.

Just recently Deek had brought out a pair of handcuffs, let Billy secure his hands behind his back, and said, "You be a tough cop and I'm a criminal who has some information you want."

Billy had played the game with a slightly drunken enthusiasm, but felt a little odd about it all when he got up the next morning, confused as to whether such a thing was right or wrong.

Deek had once again comforted him, saying, "If it's what two people want to do, and if there's no harm in it, then there's nothing wrong about doing it."

In his new life there were only a few things Billy didn't like. He wished Jameson didn't sleep in a separate bedroom. He wanted a nice warm body next to his. But Deek said he could only sleep well when he was alone. And Billy wished Deek didn't like to do so many drugs.

He never took much, but he used all kinds of stuff, and he liked Billy to join in with him. Sometimes Billy did, but often enough he faked it and flipped the capsule or tablet out of sight under the bed.

And there was one element that left him unsure, wary, but also intrigued: Billy felt their increasingly complex, sometimes ferociously intense, and fantasy-filled sex life had some definite direction. He sensed that Deek was guiding him down a road which Billy, in his inexperience, could not see. At times he wanted to pull back, but usually his fear of the unknown, which was small, only added to his sense of adventure. And so far Jameson had led him to some thrilling experiences. If these black leather chaps and vest would add to future sex scenes, then Billy would try hard to like them.

"I do like the look," he said, turning slowly in front of the mirrors and in front of Deek and the salesman.

"We'll get you an armband of black leather," Jameson said, "and three or four different pairs of boots." His voice became strained, as it always did when he was excited.

Harold had not had any sex since that last, terrible night with Billy. It had taken some time to resign himself to the idea that he was alone. He thought he might do what so many gay men did, have a new sex partner almost every time out. But he felt his life would degenerate into something without real relationships, without real meaning. He knew lots of men lived that way and thrived, but he knew as well that he wanted one single lover.

Was Frank possibly that man, Harold wondered, or was he attractive because he was a nice guy? Harold knew he was lonely too much nowadays and lately he found himself thinking of nothing but sex both awake and asleep. Frank was a great buddy. Would sex with him spoil that? It was important to Harold. He had gone out for a few beers with some of the guys at the foundry, and though they suspected nothing, he felt wary in their company, not comfortable. Once or twice one of them had tried to fix up Harold with a sister or a cousin, but Harold knew that in all of the city of San Francisco the only person he liked to be with was Frank. He didn't want to spoil that pleasant relationship with any of his personal problems. And if something happened when he went over to Frank's for dinner on Sunday, well, he'd decide what to do at the time.

With these thoughts in mind Harold dressed and readied himself for Saturday night at the Beacon, something he eagerly looked forward to each week.

At the bar Frank was busy, but he had time to wave and smile and yell greetings as Harold came in and sat down in the middle of the bar, at the only place available. And he had time to get Harold his favorite brand of beer, set it before him, make a little conversation, and admire the picture his friend made. The sleeves of Harold's red and black checked shirt were casually rolled to the elbows, displaying forearms that a lot of men wouldn't mind having as calves. . . . and that head of curly brown hair, glowing and glossy in the lamp light.

"Join the health club like you said?" Frank asked as he mixed a drink just up the bar.

"Yeah. Got me a locker not far from yours."

"Great," Frank said. All this buddy-buddy stuff was fine, especially if things worked out well on Sunday night. Harold would be the kind of lover a man would really want to keep an eye on, do everything with together.

Frank saw the other bartender become alert and curious. The customer noise volume lessened noticeably, and he knew something was happening out on the floor in the thick Saturday night crowd. Keeping himself ready for some kind of signal from the other bartender, Frank tried to see what was going on.

Two men came down the aisle along the bar to the tables in the back. One of them looked about sixty, was handsome in a worn, creased way. The man at his side was much older, white-haired and white-bearded, bent but walking without help.

As customers whispered among themselves, nodded to the two old men, and politely made way for them, Frank turned around to the bar-back and opened the drawer where he kept his personal things. He looked at the back of the dust cover of a book, closed the drawer, and turned around again.

Two young men graciously vacated a table, and both old men smiled, made their thanks, and sat down. Frank watched every move. Almost everyone else in the bar did the same and, like Frank, tried to look without appearing to stare.

Harold leaned forward to his friend and asked, very quietly, "Who are they?"

Frank explained that the younger of the two was a famous novelist, playwright, and poet.

"Oh, yeah. I've heard of him. Is he... you know?"

Frank smiled to himself at the old-fashioned expression. "Yeah, very you-know. And if you haven't heard, you're the only one who hasn't. That other guy, the real old one? That's Leighton Crane. Big

70

actor way back when, really gorgeous and, it turns out, really wild. Went to bed with almost everybody, and must have kept notes or something, because he just published his memoirs, and everyone's reading them, including me. Really tells everything, man. Like the time he went to bed with Bosie Douglas."

"Who?"

"You know, Oscar Wilde's boyfriend."

"Oh, yeah," Harold said. In truth all he knew about Oscar and Bosie came from an old movie he had seen some time ago on television, about a playwright and a trial and a young blond guy.... He found that if he sat up very straight he could see the two men's heads reflected in the bar mirror.

The floorman came to the bar with the two men's drink orders, and Frank hastened to make them. When he was done and the cocktails were on their way to the table, Harold leaned forward and said softly, "Are you sure? Oscar Wilde must have died almost a hundred years ago, maybe more."

"Douglas lived a long time afterwards. Wait." Frank took the book from its drawer. "Here. Don't let it get wet. I borrowed it from somebody."

Harold looked at the shiny, fresh cover. *A Life* was the title. He turned to the picture section and came upon a full-page photo of a young man with big eyes, dark hair and delicately-boned good looks. "At twenty — 1911" the caption read. Resisting an almost uncontrollable urge to turn around and compare the picture with the man, Harold flipped through the photo section instead, seeing the same face, young and then not so young, usually in snapshots at places that looked like they might be seaside resorts, with people he had never heard of. "With Proust and Alfredo Agostinelli — 1913," "On the set with Murnau and Conrad Veidt — Munich, 1926," "With Percy Grainger," "With R. M. Rilke." "Luncheon table, Capri, 1932. L to R Hugh Walpole, Norman Douglas, self, Somerset Maugham, Alfred Douglas."

A stir all around drew Harold's attention from the old photographs. He could see in the bar mirror that the two men were leaving. Feeling guilty, as if caught spying, he lowered the book into his lap. As they passed by he allowed himself the slightest turn of the head and the merest look. Then, again like everyone around him, after they passed on by he stared directly at them until they went out the door and stepped into a taxi at the curb.

The noise volume picked up at once, but Harold sat quiet and thoughtful, book in his hand.

Some minutes later, after the calls for refills had died down, Frank came up to Harold, who handed him back the book. "Interesting. You think he lives here?"

"Nope. Promoting the book, I bet. He's been on TV, talk shows, PBS did a program about him, like that."

Much later, near last call when the bar was relatively quiet, and Frank had time to chat without constant interruptions, Harold said, "You know, it's funny, I'm really glad those two old guys came in tonight. I never thought there was a history to it all. I mean, there has to be, but I never thought about it even once. It makes me feel, I don't know, more... real or something." He paused and an embarrassed grin spread over his face. Frank could have kissed him then and there. "Aw, I'm not making any sense."

"Sure you are," Frank said.

"Have to take your word for it, I guess," Harold said. "Well, had me a few beers and it's time for me to go. See you tomorrow, Frank."

"Right, Harold. Six at my place."

On the same night, an hour or so after the bars closed, Billy stood in Jameson's dimly lit living room. He was wearing only black leather chaps, vest, armband, cockring, and boots. The great stretch of windows framed the city's many lights into a background. Crawling toward Billy, entirely naked, was Deek Jameson.

About a yard away from Billy he stopped and raised his head. On his face was a look of worship. "Please, sir," he said, "Let me lick your boots."

"Lick my boots? Not till... not till you, uh, kiss my hand."

Jameson obeyed passionately.

Billy felt relieved, figuring he had the general idea of this game now. He noticed that Deek was becoming more and more excited, now busy lapping at the boots and mumbling in a growling monotone.

Feeling a little silly, Billy stood in the huge, shadowy room and wished he found this sort of stuff even half as interesting as Deek did.

Around four in the morning Warren woke up in his cubicle at the steambaths. He felt a little woozy from the grass he had smoked during the several hours of action before his nap. Wrapping his towel around his waist and giving his darkly red hair a quick combing, he went outside and through the labyrinth of hallways to a comfortably furnished lounge. He bought a cup of coffee out of a vending machine,

72

settled in a chair, and gazed indifferently at the grey and ancient late-late movie on the television set.

Twenty minutes later Warren made his way to a dark room that was all pillowed and carpeted. He put his towel around his neck and moved toward one corner and its pile of hard-breathing male bodies. A hand came forth, and then another. They pulled him closer. Willingly, Warren allowed himself to be absorbed into the anonymous mass.

"Real nice dinner," Harold said as he settled onto the couch in Frank's bay-windowed living room. It was Sunday night.

"Thanks," Frank replied, coming out of the kitchen with a tray in his hands. "I've brought a couple of after-dinner drinks." He set the tray on the coffee table and handed Harold a glass full of gently tinkling ice, a lot of gin, and a little tonic.

Frank put a country and western record on his stereo and sat down on the couch next to Harold. Casually he checked the lighting in the living room. It seemed just right, neither too bright and glaring nor too shadowy and dim. And he checked out his guest: Harold was sitting rather stiffly and looked a little nervous.

Maybe Harold was more lonely than interested, but Frank was determined to change that. He knew he had been a straight shooter while Billy was in the picture, but now everything was different.

"Hey, let's dance," Frank said.

"Well, I don't know. Never did it with a man."

"Come on, let's take a couple of spins around the living room." With that, Frank tugged a grinning Harold to his feet.

When they were facing each other Harold began to giggle. "I hope you'll let me lead," he said. "I don't have any idea how to follow."

"Okay," Frank said. "Just so you don't think I'm a fag for following."

Waiting for the beat, Harold started tentatively, but soon the couple was gliding in waltz time around the room with little difficulty.

When the song ended they stopped to wait for the next one, taking advantage of the brief silence to sip at their drinks.

"No offense, Frank, but I think we probably look kind of like Mutt and Jeff."

"This one's a foxtrot." They started to dance again, and Frank went on: "Maybe we do look a little like Laurel and Hardy, but so what? As long as we're having fun, what the hell."

"Right."

"Hey, maybe some Sunday afternoon we can go dancing. I know a couple of country-western dance bars."

"They let men dance together?" Harold asked, surprised.

"Sure. They're gay places."

"Oh. I was thinking—"

"Right," Frank said.

After dancing a while, they retired to the couch and made quiet conversation. One of Frank's hands strayed up to the back of the couch and the fingers came to rest on Harold's far shoulder. After a while, as if unconsciously, the digits softly but steadily massaged the base of Harold's neck.

In a short time Harold stopped talking, grinned bashfully, and put his hand on top of Frank's, to stop the movements on his neck.

"Bother you?" Frank asked, voice low and quiet. He liked having his hand flattened under the huge, rough-palmed hand of his Goliath.

"Well, not exactly. Just kinda gets to me."

"Anything wrong with that?"

Harold saw a beautiful young blond man's face, just for a moment, and pushed the sight away. That was over. There was no going back. "No, I don't guess so... feels real nice."

"Guess you know I'm putting on the make. I don't plan to stop, either. Anyway, you're bigger and stronger than I am, you can take care of yourself."

"I... sometimes I'm a little shy about all this kind of thing," Harold said, as if making a dark confession or telling Frank something he hadn't already picked up on. With that the big hand came away from the little one and went from neck to the drink on the coffee table. Taking a big swallow, Harold went on: "I could do something too, but I just don't know what, exactly."

"I'll keep you posted," Frank said softly. "For now, just relax and let me make you feel real nice." He began to massage Frank's neck more deeply than before, and at the same time he slid his other hand inside Harold's red flannel XL shirt. Frank drew his fingers along the underside of the big man's right pectoral, where the flesh lay firm and smooth and the breast stood out in hard, distinct relief against the chest. Frank cupped the firm musculature for a time, enjoying its warmth and the fast fluttering heartbeats. Then two fingers searched out and captured the nipple, a thick, round column.

"Ohhh," Harold breathed. "That feels really good.... Nobody ever did that to me before."

Surprised, Frank realized just how limited Harold's experience with

74

men really was. The sensitive nipple held in his caressing fingers was stiff now, and Frank could sense momentary trembles and shivers in Harold's body, making his voice uneven as he sighed. He looked in his friend's eyes and saw nervousness. Mustn't panic, Frank thought. Just slow down a little, so he won't panic. Just—

As Harold moved, his unbuttoned shirt slid aside from his wide expanse of chest, and Frank felt himself buried in a hairy bearhug. Then irresistible arms pulled him upward. As Harold's face met Frank's they kissed, lightly once or twice, and then ferociously, their shaven cheeks scraping each other.

But he was fearful that now matters were moving ahead too fast. Frank pressed Harold back against the couch pillows, then dug down between the two thighs, huge and firm in taut denim, and massaged Harold's hardening, impressive meat. As he worked he spoke softly into Harold's ear: "Just take it easy now... there's no rush... that's right... let me loosen your belt... get at those fly buttons... there...."

Frank slid to his knees, crouching half under the coffee table, put his hands at the sensitive juncture of Harold's thighs and his torso, and bent down toward the gleamingly erect member standing forth from the gaping blue jeans. Then he exhaled a slow stream of his warm breath on it, and two big hands suddenly took powerful grip of his shoulders. Frank looked up at Harold, who gasped, "I'm afraid I'll— you know."

Held away from the object he wanted most at that moment, Frank extended his tongue as far as it would reach, and the tip touched the head. Frank slowly moved it all around the hot, hard, rounded surface. When the power that held him began to waver Frank took the advantage to run his exploring tongue down the large crevice in the head, then slowly snaked it down the red flesh of the shaft and back up again.

Frank heard a sigh and a groan from above, and the hands holding him seemed to forget their strength, then fall away. At once he sank his mouth down onto Harold and set to work, using everything he knew.

Soon Frank found himself tightly held between powerful legs that turned him this way and that as Harold twisted and writhed all over the couch. He worked harder and harder, and in a short time he felt Harold's body stiffen, then arch upward. Frank held tight around his friend's body and kept up his action, now moving faster and faster. When he felt that certain jutting throb on the lower side of the cock, he redoubled his grip and slid his throat down over Harold's meat. Frank pressed downward until his teeth were buried in rich, dark pubic hair. He swallowed as hard as he could, again and again, until he heard, as if from far away, a sound between a heavy groan and a stifled yell. He felt the juice blowing hard and thick. Frank raised up and sucked, harder and harder, until nothing more would come and Harold was begging him to stop.

They rested. Harold half-lay flung out against the couch, spread-legged and breathing as if he'd run the marathon. Frank came up from the floor to join him.

When they had caught their breaths, Frank suggested they undress. Harold shucked his clothes with no hesitation, which made his host smile to himself. They finished their drinks and began to kiss and fool around. "Hey, why don't you take off your clothes too?" Harold asked. "Got your shirt off, how about your pants?"

Frank stood up and took a stance in front of Harold, nudging the big man's knees apart so he could stand between Harold's legs.

That's when Harold saw that Frank's tight, faded jeans had a dark, wet spot in the crotch.

Frank flipped the fly buttons loose with two fingers and pulled out his cock. It was dark and semi-erect, with its foreskin half closed over the head, which shone with a large drop of ejaculate. Frank touched the thick liquid with one finger. "Tonight's just a start," he said, "and this time was just a start for tonight." He held out his finger, burden gleaming on its tip, toward Harold. "We can go a long way, but as far as we go, it'll be at your speed. No problems, no more than you can handle." He raised his finger to Harold's lips. "Taste mine," he said softly.

How strange this all is, Harold thought, but how sexy, and how right. . . . He touched his lower lip to Frank's finger and tasted a sweet saltiness. He raised his hands to caress the wiry, beautifully made body that stood right in front of him. The finger make its way into his mouth and gently caressed his tongue. Harold felt his cock stir again. He felt he was going into a world he had never known existed, and with a man who obviously knew the territory. Stiffening again as the wet finger traced a path down his cheek and neck to one of his nipples, Harold at that moment wanted to spend every minute of his life having sex with Frank, any way Frank wanted him and any time.

8

Softly diffused late morning light added to the pleasantness of Billy's bedroom. He lay awake and wished he could have gone on sleeping, so he would not have to face the memories of the night before. They were not entirely clear but still managed to be sharply painful.

He knew he had been wearing his black leather clothes and nothing else. They had smoked grass and taken some sort of pills. Deek, naked, had been reeling about, or maybe they both were. Billy wasn't sure. He did remember the belt, a wide length of black leather, the belt that apparently floated into Billy's hand. He had chased Deek around the huge living room, beating him as he ran, beating him more when, trapped among pieces of furniture, he knelt cowering. How long had he whipped Deek's bare back and ass? Billy shuddered.

A beautiful thought came dancing into his mind: maybe all he had done, or most of it, had been a dream. Maybe Deek's vivid talk had become dramatized inside Billy's head. No... it had not been a dream. It had been all too real.

There was a knock at the door. Billy sat up at once, ready for the police or at the least a furious, injured Deek. "Come in."

The door opened to reveal a smiling Deek Jameson. "Good morning, my dear boy. How are you?"

"Fine," Billy answered, amazed at Deek's cheeriness. "Are you... all right?"

"Never better, you little devil."

"But, last night. I think I got carried away and—"

"Billy, I'm trying to tell you that it was charming, lovely, delightful. And to think I'd ever meet anyone as wildly wonderful as you in a place as common as the Beacon. Life is just amazing. Come, breakfast with me. It's a lovely day. I do believe the fogs are over for the year, and we're in for a warm, beautiful late summer."

Billy got out of bed, much relieved, and put on his robe. He would have used none of Deek's words to describe the events of the night before, and he was surprised at Jameson's remark about the Beacon.

Much later that day, at a cocktail party in the hills of Marin County, Billy gazed from the deck toward San Francisco, its hills pallid with buildings, and wondered just how far Deek would want him to go with these sex games. Well, maybe I didn't really hurt him, Billy thought, maybe it was just more pretending.... I hope so.

When Warren went into the Beacon on Friday night, he found someone besides Frank behind the bar. "Gary, hi. I thought you worked at the Phoenix."

"Still do. Just filling in."

"Frank sick?" Warren asked.

"Off on a long weekend with that huge mound of muscle he's been going with."

"Oh, Harold."

"That his name? Well, they went down to the Sur."

Warren sipped his drink and thought of Frank, so admirable for his persistence, now taking his love down to the mountains and trees and ocean of the Big Sur. He thought Frank was setting himself up for a big ugly painful fall. Warren tried to think of somebody he'd like to spend a weekend with, but he could only come up with names from the past. But all that was many searing burns ago. He was surprised at how much appeal the idea had for him, spending a weekend in some beautiful place with one special man. Or maybe, he thought, I'm just getting a little mushy in my middle thirties.

Early on Saturday morning Frank and Harold left the cabin in the

78

state park where they had stayed over Friday night, and went on south in the car Frank had rented. Harold had never seen such spectacular scenery, heavily forested mountains sloping steeply to the highway, and to their right the steep, often cliff-like drops to the Pacific Ocean hundreds of feet below.

"Really beautiful," Harold said. "I didn't realize last night in the dark."

"We could have got here sooner," Frank replied, "but I thought it'd be nice to have a seafood dinner on the wharf in Monterey."

"Yeah, that was nice. California sure is pretty."

"We're seeing it at the best time of the year. Winters can be cold and stormy down here."

Some miles further south they pulled into a little rustic motel-cafe-gas station. As the attendant filled the tank, Frank took a little piece of paper from his pocket, unfolded it, and showed it to Harold.

"A friend says if we follow this map we can get to a really deserted area. Has a beach and everything."

"Sounds fine to me," Harold said.

Carefully following landmarks, several miles down the highway Frank turned off at a dirt track that carried them downward, slowly and bumpily, to a flat area of reeds, brush, and sand. They took their gear out of the car and followed a stream some hundreds of yards to a bluff of dark, weathered rock, then made their way down the cliff with care and reached a deep half-moon cove.

They found dunes and a pond of calm water in an indentation to the north. "We can camp here, above the pool. Looks so clean. Must have filled up from a super high tide. And the dunes will protect us from the wind."

They set up a little camp of sleeping bags, supplies, water and food. Afterwards, Harold stood admiring the world around him, the towering cliffs behind, the ocean in front. "Sure is noisy," he said. "I'll bet it's too dangerous to swim, though."

Frank looked at the rollers dashing spray as they broke over huge, weather-sculpted rocks just off the shoreline, and he said, "You're right. And it's really cold, too. But the pool looks okay, maybe warmed from the sun. Want to take a swim?"

"Sure."

Frank began undressing. As he slipped off his jeans he said, "Since there's not a soul around here except you and me, I don't think we need to worry about swim suits and all that."

The idea made Harold a little nervous. But he was in a world that seemed hardly connected to any reality he had ever known — incredible giant-scale scenery, the endless, booming ocean, and no sign of human life — and when he, slowly stripping off his shirt and T shirt, saw Frank naked and gleaming against the paleness of the sand dunes, he knew nothing was more right. And nothing was more beautiful. What a guy, Frank.

Harold tore off his clothes, and the two men splashed into the sandy-bottomed pool.

They found the water bearable, if not warm, and they swam and played for some time. Then they spread a blanket on the flank of a sand dune and lay down to dry and rest in the sun.

The night before, in the cabin, they had rolled all over the rug in front of the fireplace, wrestling and laughing and making love in the firelight. The fire had burned to embers before they had satisfied each other and themselves enough finally to go to sleep

Now, in the afternoon, lying nude in the sunlight, they felt first rested and then revitalized. Frank and Harold touched hands, then turned toward each other and brought their warm, salt-streaked bodies together in a strong embrace.

When they were exhausted again, they took a quick, cleansing dip in the pond, ate sandwiches and milk they'd brought along, then lay down again.

Frank could not sleep, so he got up on one elbow and gazed down on Harold, his face beautifully composed in the innocent expression of the sleeper. Love for Harold welled up enormously in Frank, love and the intense desire to have Harold love him back. He hoped this weekend would help Harold see with new eyes, the two of them alone in this wild place, just themselves and nature.

Frank unfolded another old blanket and gently draped it over Harold's naked body. The wind had grown stronger and cooler. Frank felt the need to move about, so he strolled from one end of their little universe to the other, along the crescent of beach to the tidepools on the south, where the cliffs jutted far into the tideline, indifferent to the furiously battering waves.

When Harold awoke he found Frank, now wearing only a T shirt, sitting on the blanket beside him.

"I was just about to wake you," Frank said. "Look." He pointed out toward the ocean.

Harold sat up and put his arm around Frank. He watched in awe as the sky's blue slowly turned into an array of gorgeous tints. They saw the last orange bit of the sun disappear. The colors in the sky grew fainter but no less beautiful, then died away into blackness, with only a thin slash of glare remaining along the horizon. Even that soon evaporated and all the world was sea and stars.

"It's less cold now," Harold said as he stood up, rising naked out of the blankets on the dune.

"Wind's died down," Frank said. "But we better put on some clothes."

Wearing jeans and T shirts, they built a small fire in the valley formed by three sand dunes, and its heat felt delicious. Their inexperience and the lack of certain essential utensils they should have brought turned dinner preparation into a comic masterpiece. They tramped around the fire in the cold sand, laughing and joking all the while. When it was at last ready, the food tasted very good.

Afterwards they took a short walk and then moved their blankets and goods over the dune and down to the campfire. They lay half-sitting, drinking cans of beer and gazing at the sky, which now was thickly littered with an immense number of bright stars.

"Look at the Milky Way," Frank said.

"Yeah...."

"That's the rest of the galaxy that we're in."

"Wow.... I've felt so little and tiny all day, and now I feel like just a speck.... And those stars over there, way to the left? Don't they exactly form a big letter B?"

B for Billy, Frank thought. Still on his mind. What he thinks about in those peculiar silences that take him over, when he drifts away, looks sad.... Why can't he see an F in the goddamned sky?

"Mmm," was all Frank replied.

Not long afterwards they decided it was definitely getting cold, so they unrolled their sleeping bags, zipped them together to form a single sleeping space, undressed and slipped inside the cool, thickly padded bedrolls.

Bodies together, they quickly warmed up, and in a short time they were making love. Frank brought Harold along to the point of total abandon, and he found that he too was out of control. Abstractly he knew that he was going to do something Harold disliked, but he desired it himself so hotly that he felt it impossible to do anything but go on.

As they kissed furiously, Frank pushed his hand under Harold's meat, dug one finger deep between his buns, and touched a very sensitive place.

Harold reacted with muscle contractions there and in his loins, but he did not try to stop Frank this time. When Frank's finger ceased its hypnotic explorations and entered Harold, there was no objection, only a brief grunting sound.

Using the tube of lubricant he had with him, Frank worked carefully, trying to give the maximum erotic sensation with the least possible amount of pain.

Harold was groaning and bucking, all the while clinging tightly to Frank.

After a while, Frank suddenly jerked his finger out of Harold, who emitted something between a sigh and a groan. Frank forcefully turned Harold on his stomach, and struggling in the confined space of the two joined sleeping bags, he got on top of Harold. Frank entered Harold as gently as he could. Nearly overwhelmed with pleasure, he fought off the desire to come, and resolutely worked both to make the moment last and to give Harold as much pleasure as possible, with the least pain.

Shortly, overcome by his body's overpowering desire, Frank clung tightly to the seething musculature of the man beneath him and let the inevitable happen. And he played it for all it was worth, knowing he had maybe spoiled everything and that this could easily be the last as well as first time. Regret entered Frank's mind well before the last of passion died away. He expressed it to Harold by gentleness and concern while they washed at the now icy pond.

Frank wasn't sure what to make of Harold's silence. They returned to the sleeping bag as if nothing had happened, and cuddled up together, spoon style, Frank deep in Harold's arms and pressed against his chest.

"Frank?" came a whisper in his ear.

"Yeah?"

"It's my turn."

"Your turn," Frank said, considering the matter. "Right. It is your turn. . . . The lube's around some— here it is."

Frank usually didn't care to be the bottom, so it was not easy to take Harold, who wasn't too experienced in any case, and who was healthily built. But afterwards Frank felt pleasured, good. Harold was the right man, so it was fine, fine, fine. . . .

Washed again and back in the sleeping bag, close-held bodies shivering together, Harold said in a low soft voice, "You know, I have to admit something: I didn't think you'd do it for me. I thought it was maybe just a trick, and that made me feel real bad, coming from you. But it wasn't, and now I feel bad for having all those doubts."

"It's just another way to love," Frank said. "Nothing wrong with it, long as we make each other feel good doing it."

"Yeah... it does feel good, both ways, Frank. Hurts some to get it, but... it does feel good.... I thought I'd feel ashamed, but I don't. And I guess you're right, it is just one more way to love."

Frank lay in Harold's arms, back against his hard, hairy chest, and listened for Harold to say more, something else with the word 'love' in it. After a short wait what he heard was the steady rhythms of a man breathing while deeply asleep.

In San Francisco that Saturday night, at ten o'clock — the same time that Frank and Harold were falling asleep down in the Sur — Warren was combing and dressing with great care. He was preparing to do something he hadn't bothered with in years. Warren was going to go to the bars and try to meet somebody. Not just a trick, but someone who would be worth getting to know better.

"This is folly," he said to himself in the full length mirror on the inside of his bedroom closet door. "I know," Warren replied to himself, "But it should be amusing... and what the hell: people do meet people from time to time. And the baths are open all night if nothing works out, and it probably won't."

Warren carried some clothes out to the car and headed it northwest, to an old and nicely gentrified part of the city. L'Atelier presented a quiet frontage just across the street from a handsome Victorian relic of a park. Warren went in and felt he was in an art deco womb: dark blue carpeting, an undulating bar of blond wood, chairs and tables on several levels, and exquisitely considerate lighting.

The drinks had prices to match the thoughtfulness of the decor.

"Warren, it's you!"

"Trevor, well hello!" Warren looked fondly at a man about thirty years old, with pleasant features and sandy hair. Trevor had been the lover of a mutual friend who had moved east some months before.

"Warren, it's so good to see you again. Frankly, I always thought you were so charming. Redheads do things to me, anyway, but — where did you get that lovely tweed jacket?"

"The usual place," Warren said.

"The brothers, yes. So dependable. Can't wait for them to have a sale."

"You're looking very good yourself, Trevor. Still single?"

"Yes, curse it. But I'm so busy now, done so many interiors, just heaps. One of them won an award, just local but always nice. And I just got back from a vacation — had to take six weeks or go merely bonkers — in Acapulco. I had the most marvelous time and I met these people who are just fascinating. He's a count and she's a duchess, or maybe the other way around. Anyway. . . ."

Warren listened politely for six or eight minutes more, and with each second that passed he felt less and less interested in the man. Trevor had been a good deal more interesting when he had been somebody else's lover. Politely Warren excused himself to go to the bathroom. He saw a flicker of disappointment in Trevor's eyes. Warren knew that under certain circumstances he might let his ear be talked off in return for a bout of sex. But there was no use listening endlessly, considering that tonight he wanted some higher possibilities of communication.

He went from the bathroom to the car, then drove to a nearby place, on a commercial street, another bar he hadn't been to before. He sipped his scotch and observed the crowd. By and large it consisted of young men in attire suitable for a college campus and older men in grey slacks and blazers. The latter were buying drinks for the former.

Paying for it, Warren told himself, is not exactly what I had in mind for tonight. He finished his drink and left.

Some miles south and west Warren parked on a small residential street on a hillside. When he got out of the car his slacks and jacket were folded on the back seat, and he was wearing a short denim jacket, polo shirt, and close-fitting jeans. Sauntering down the hill to Market Street, he walked a block or two to Castro Street and went into one of its many gay bars.

Twenty minutes later Warren was deep in conversation with a man he judged to be about his own age. Cary was from his own state, back east, and gave all indications of being interesting and intelligent, besides sexy. Warren therefore encouraged him to talk about himself, and he did. But he asked Warren about himself from time to time, and even if Warren minimized personal chat, he felt Cary's interest in him showed a definite degree of class.

Cary confided that he was a little unhappy. "Broke up with a really wonderful guy. Looks, style, and smart too. I just adored him. But . . . one of those things. You have a lover?"

"No," Warren replied.

"Well, maybe you and I could — Oh! Excuse me!"

Cary's sudden panic and his dash from the back of the bar toward the entrance gave Warren quite a surprise. He watched him talking fast to another man who had just come in — quite young, rather oddly pretty in a spoiled-child way, and wearing incredibly tight jeans and T shirt. His hair was short and of a blond color that never existed in nature.

As he watched the two men argued, then went out of the bar together. Warren left a few minutes later, wondering if that young man was the lost love that Cary had described as having looks, style, and brains.

Several bars and men later, including a charming guy who turned out to be married to a woman and terrified that any of his straight friends might find out about him, Warren gave up.

Feeling a little woozy from the quantity of cocktails he had drunk, Warren went home and to bed. He lay talking to himself as if he were two people, something he commonly did when he had some matter to figure out, some personal knot to be untied.

One after another, they become impossible for you. Every damn one of them. Okay, leaving aside the one whose lover came back, why were they all unsuitable at the end, however good they looked at the beginning? That's a pattern, so what is its meaning?

Everyone is wearing armor, everyone has his guard up. Real communication is almost impossible.

Well, maybe, but there's more to it than that. The pattern is too consistent. It comes down to you rejecting them, doesn't it?

I guess it does.

And your armor was in place, too. Don't fool yourself about that.

Wrong. I went out open to the world.

Hah. You went out and you gave everybody enough conversational rope, and every one of them, almost, chattered himself into the noose right in front of you. . . . Maybe some of them talked so much because you said so little. How much did you really give, darling, and how much did you hold back?

With that the dialogue ceased, because Warren saw how he was still locked inside his own high granite walls of self-protection, and he saw how he had, all unknowing, arranged for the world to prove disappointing.

Maybe I learned something tonight, he thought as he drifted closer to sleep. Maybe fast-food sex is the answer for me. Maybe anything else is psychologically impossible. . . .

For Billy life had been quiet for some days now. Deek had a summer cold, and beyond nursing him a little, there was little for Billy to do.

On Saturday Deek felt better and on Sunday he said he was just fine. That afternoon he said to Billy, "There's something I've decided I should show you. Come along."

Billy followed Jameson down to the end of the little-used hall that passed behind the kitchen and ended in a window that opened onto a fire escape. Deek unlocked a door which Billy had hardly noticed and always assumed to be a closet. Jameson stepped inside and signaled Billy to follow.

A few paces and Billy found himself in a room whose walls were painted black. What light there was came from red globes. Chains hung from it, ending in cuffs of black leather.

Deek guided an amazed Billy to an ornate chest of drawers. He opened one, exposing a number of whips inside. The second drawer contained a lot of different kinds of restraints, of leather, rubber, and chain. The items in the third drawer, variously of metal and leather and rope, some with large fishing weights attached, merely confused Billy. He could make no sense of the sinister looking mass.

Deek slowly closed the last drawer, turned to Billy and asked him, "Tell me, dear boy, how do you feel?"

"Feel? Well... um... sort of strange, I guess."

"Billy, ever since the night when you used the belt on me, on my bare buttocks, all over my body, I've thought of revealing this room to you. You are young, inexperienced, but I think you have the true feeling for all this inside you."

More puzzled than ever, Billy said, "Deek, do you mind if we leave? I really don't feel comfortable in here, not at all."

"Leave? But of course, Billy." In the hall Deek went on: "Let me just lock this door securely... there. Billy, perhaps you don't understand. You must never think that I want to hurt you. The aggressive role is yours... and I am the one who would have to take chances...."

Billy said, "Deek, I just don't like any of that stuff, not even like the other night, and the chaps and all that. I really don't like a bit of it."

"Ah.... I must have misunderstood many things." Deek was silent for a few moments. Then he said, "Billy, my dear, very few people know anything about that room. I trust you'll mention it to nobody."

"I promise," Billy said.

"Forget about all this. We won't speak of it again."

"Not a word, Deek," Billy said, happy that Deek understood his feelings so well.

9

It was a busy Friday night at the Beacon but Warren, who had not been in the place all week, had a chance to ask Frank how his long weekend had gone.

The bartender, deeply tanned, looked up and said, "Not bad at all. . . . Hey, Hal and I are going to a party after closing, mostly bartenders. Why don't you come with us?"

"Sure. Sounds good."

After Frank finished up behind the bar, he and Harold and Warren walked a few blocks up an almost quiet Polk Street, now populated mostly by young men out hustling, and went up a half block on Clay to a handsome old apartment house.

In the elevator Frank said, "Almost all bartenders living here, so it's pretty alive after hours."

"Now I know what bartenders do after work: party," Warren said.

"Right, man. It's a little hard to go to a bar or out dancing."

They followed Frank out of the elevator and down the hall to a door.

The room within was full of men, talking and smoking joints, dancing and kissing. A single lamp with a red globe illuminated the scene. To Harold it all looked rather wicked and attractive at the same time.

Their host brought them drinks. The record player music changed to something slow and smooth. Harold asked Frank to dance, feeling very daring about it. They moved slowly to the soothing rhythms, glad to be deep in each other's embrace, enjoying their purring desire and half-hardness.

Frank knew he was drunk with love for Harold. He knew it could be fatal to admit his feelings, but he could sense all restraint weakening. He would say the words, whatever the consequences, he was sure; maybe in a day or two, maybe much sooner, but they would come out no matter what.

Harold had everything in his heart for Frank except that final and complete feeling that nothing and nobody else mattered. It was the feeling that made it perfectly right to tear up years of a life, end a marriage, leave job and hometown, and move to a strange city half a country away. Harold suspected such a bout of madness was never to occur again, that the experience of it protected him from any repetition.

Even when the cartridge needle silently passed through the spaces between songs, the couple continued their slow dance. When the host turned the record over or changed it for another, they stood in place, holding each other, until the music, which was always slow, came on again.

Frank and Harold hardly realized it, but after a while they were dancing by themselves, Frank with his head against Harold's chest, Frank's curly hair warming Harold's cheek.

Across the room, gathered with the others on the couch and chairs in a corner, Warren chatted blandly and from time to time watched his friends as they danced, thinking as always that they were only setting themselves up for pain and unhappiness. Still, he had a good feeling, a warmth that contradicted his reasoning. His friends were happy... now, and they made a beautiful picture.

The host, next to Warren, commented on the dancers they were both looking at: "Shows that love comes in all sizes."

Warren nodded and smiled, realizing he was not the only one at this gathering who had noticed Harold and Frank.

One of the other guests said, "One of them looks like the box the other came in."

"Yes, but they're both such nice packages," the host said.

"And they dance well together," another guest added.

"If you can call that dancing," said a young, attractive bartender known for his wicked mouth. "I think I'd say they *throb* well together."

The host cut off any further remarks, saying, "Love is so pretty to watch, don't you think?"

By words and nods the others agreed. One of the guests raised a can of beer in a silent toast, and the others followed suit.

Across the room Harold no longer felt confused or doubtful. Everything was strongly focused for him now. He moved his face downward against the side of Frank's head.

"I love you," Harold said. He was surprised to feel that he had just grabbed hold of a wire full of electricity. Frank would laugh, go away, make fun of him, make light of what he said. How could I be so stupid, he thought, how could I embarrass myself like this? What have I done, what have I—?

"I love you too, man," Frank said softly, head raised against Harold's face.

The lovers held each other all the more tightly and wished the present would freeze, would last throughout eternity. As their fright left them and joy took its place, their hearts fluttered into high gear, and each could feel the other's against his chest.

Slowly they went on dancing, unaware of anything but each other.

When the record ended they stopped, separated for the first time in an hour, and in rather dazed states each said his good night.

The host saw them to the door, then watched them as they went up the hall to the elevator. When he came back to his guests the sharp-tongued young man asked, "And did they float all the way down the hall, too?"

The host answered, "I believe they did."

"Isn't love wonderful?" the young man said. "Really reduces wear and tear on rugs."

Warren finished his drink, lecturing himself all the while: I see two nice guys who are getting it on, and I think I'm missing something, so I get all puddly. Which is what this nonsense I'm feeling is all about.

Though he kept repeating this thought over and over, it was not as comforting as he hoped it would be. Somewhere, somehow, something in it rang false.

Warren's thoughts were interrupted suddenly as the young, fast-mouthed bartender, sitting next to him, burst into tears.

Billy awoke on a deck chair in the apartment's central patio. He was groggy, drugged with late summer's afternoon sunshine. Staggering inside and to his bedroom, he toweled off the remaining suntan lotion and fell into bed.

Many hours later he woke up again, now feeling much better. Billy reflected that he hadn't been getting all the sleep he needed lately. He took a quick shower and dressed in his bathrobe, then went to find Deek and explain why he hadn't done any work in the office.

As Billy padded barefoot down the hall carpet toward the living room, two voices came to him, quiet but clear. He stopped; one of the two men talking was Deek's friend Quentin, the guy with the yacht. Billy had met him a number of times lately and had grown to thoroughly dislike the man, particularly his lecherously probing eyes.

Billy decided he would retreat and wait until Quentin was gone. But then he heard his own name mentioned and he stopped.

"Billy could come with me on the yacht," Quentin's voice said. "I think he'd be excellent company for my three-month cruise of the South Seas. That might be the best way to settle the matter."

"Perhaps it would after all," Deek said, much to Billy's surprise. "I do hate scenes with these young men, especially with the ones who tend to be rather... clinging. Well then, I'll bring Billy out to the yacht on Saturday morning next. You will have Nelson for me in exchange, and while you sail off for tropical dalliance, I shall be amusing myself with Nelson here."

"Sounds good to me," Quentin said.

"You guarantee that Nelson *is* interested in my kinds of sex?"

"Deek, young as he is, Nelson is kinkier than a corkscrew, not to my taste at all. And you say that Billy is not into S&M?"

"I was so fascinated by his looks," Jameson said, "and I hoped I could bring him along. But then, last week when I showed him the blackroom he was, well, hardly intrigued.... Quite a disappointment."

"And what if our little trade doesn't work out?" Quentin asked.

"I suggest a mutual hustler-back guarantee," Jameson said.

"Excellent. Then it's a deal. Let us seal it with a drink."

Billy wanted to hear no more. He fled down the hall to his room, threw on the nearest clothes, and went the back way down to the street.

He knew it must be quite late and regretted not having thought to bring his wristwatch. The streets were almost empty of traffic, and even near the huge hotels of Nob Hill pedestrians and taxis were few.

Billy didn't care. His brain was afire with what he had heard. All Deek's words, all his understanding and kindness, everything was fake. The man he thought of as his lover looked on him as a thing, a toy, to be traded for another toy. No, Deek looked on him as a hustler. That hurt even more.

Billy knew it was over with Deek and that he would never have anything to do with Quentin. What he would do was totally unclear, something he could not think about clearly with his mind in such turmoil.

California Street suddenly blocked his way. He could cross it and go on down the south side of Nob Hill, into the Tenderloin again, and find a room in some grim hotel. Or he could walk down to the Beacon and see Frank, have a beer, feel human warmth. Billy turned right and started down Californis Street. Maybe Frank would know of some inexpensive hotel on Polk or near it, which would be safer than the Tenderloin at this late hour.

Several blocks further west, Billy realized that Harold might be in the Beacon. Harold would be more than he could handle at this desperate time. Billy decided he would check out the bar first from outside, instead of just going right on in.

He reached the Beacon in a short time and cautiously peeked through the window. Being somewhat uphill from the entrance level, Billy could see a good deal of the interior. He recognized Warren, red hair and all, at his usual place down at the end of the bar, and he saw Frank too. Sitting at the bar with his back to the windows was a big man with sturdy shoulders and a head of dark, curly hair. Billy didn't need to see the face to know who it was.

The Beacon was not to be his refuge tonight, he realized. Just as Billy was about to turn away, he saw Frank laugh, then lean across the bar and give the big man a hug and a kiss. They both were returned fully.

Billy was amazed. Harold must have changed a lot in the last few months if he was kissing men in plain sight in public places. Kissing Frank. Harold and Frank! Only now, and with a sharp jab of pain, did Billy realize that Harold might have gone on to become involved with someone else. . . with Frank.

Fighting back tears, Billy tried to think of what to do now. He decided to go on down to Polk Street, find a cheap hotel if he could, or one of the relatively expensive motels on Van Ness Avenue if necessary. But he would not pass the Beacon. He would go back up California, cross to the other side, and make his way to Polk Street from there.

He turned away from the sight of the warm, pleasant bar and started up California Street.

"Faggot!"

The sound came from a narrow alley, and it seemed to have been screamed in his ear just an instant before a hard fist hit his jaw.

Billy was stunned. Stumbling, he fought to escape, but numerous hands dragged him into the dark alley. He tried to protect himself as his attackers punched him and called him names, then kicked him after he fell to the wet pavement.

Suddenly he was alone. With the aid of a garbage can and a solid brick wall he managed to get to his feet. He knew he was bleeding, he could taste the thick, sweet saltiness in his mouth. With throbs of pain coming from all over his body, Billy staggered toward the glow of California Street. The moment he reached the sidewalk and tried to stand on his own, the world began to slip and turn at all kinds of crazy angles. Billy felt himself running, sliding downhill, and flying all at once, as in a dream. He could not see for all the sparkling masses of color in the way. Then everything, the fear, the pain, all receded infinitely, further and further until there was nothing but a pinpoint of light in total blackness....

Quentin left Deek's apartment in an excellent mood. He could hardly wait to get that Billy alone and get his pants off. And Deek, he thought, had been so eager. That magazine with those bondage pictures of Nelson, made a year or so ago, before Nelson began peddling his ass, that clinched it, Quentin was sure. And Deek, so worried everyone would find out about his masochistic desires. How silly, when everyone knew anyway.... Ah well, deal set, and Quentin looked forward to having Billy's pale young body under him once or twice a day every day for the next six months or so, until Billy's charms no longer interested him very much....

10

Billy woke up slowly, at first aware only that he was lying in a bed, not on a sidewalk. Then, as he looked around he discovered he was in a very familiar room. And standing over the bed was somebody he knew well.

"Harold!" Billy said, his words coming out in a croak. "I mean, Harold. What...? How did I get here in your apartment?"

"After the emergency room, we didn't know where to take you. No information in your wallet, and you weren't very talkative."

The words "emergency room" brought back a wild mass of memories, of fists coming out of nowhere, harsh young male voices yelling "Faggot! Faggot!", of people dressed in white, of pills coming at him in a paper cup.... Billy looked down at himself. White gauze was taped in two places on his left arm. He had a number of scrapes and bruises on his chest. He looked up and strained to see himself in the dresser mirror across the room.

"I— Do you have a little mirror?" he asked Harold.

"Sure," Harold said, and brought one from the bathroom.

Billy saw a young man in the reflection with a somewhat swollen left cheek, cuts and scrapes here and there, and a very large black eye. "Wow," he said.

"Guess you got mugged, right?" Harold asked gently.

"Yeah... some guys came out of that little alley... just up from the Beacon?"

Harold nodded. "Hey, you want something to eat, some breakfast?"

"Uh... I don't think so. Feel kind of queasy. But thanks."

Billy spoke the truth, but he felt embarrassed to be in this situation. At least Harold was being very plain and relaxed about his generosity. Well, for all his shortcomings, Hal has always been a kind person, Billy thought.

"Listen," Harold said. "You have a visitor. Think you can hack a little company?"

Billy felt a sudden attack of panic as he pictured Deek coming through the door. "Well, who is it?"

"Frank," Harold said. "He was a big help last night, getting you to the emergency room at the hospital, then he helped me get you back here."

Frank, your lover, Billy thought. "I'd love to see him," he said, not quite truthfully.

Harold nodded and left the room, and very shortly came back in, following a smiling Frank.

"Hi, Billy. How are you doing this morning?"

"Okay. Hal tells me you were a big help... thanks."

"Sure."

"Hal says I was in a hospital emergency room and all, but I just faintly remember a few things."

"It'll come back after a while," Frank said. "You did get hit in the head, so...."

"They did X-rays on you," Harold said, "but they couldn't find any internal injuries, so you don't have to worry about that."

"They did think you should stay overnight," Frank went on, "but we figured you didn't have any medical insurance, so we thought it'd be cheaper this way. They said all we had to do was keep an eye on you, bring you back if you got sick to your stomach or dizzy or something." Frank didn't want to repeat all the danger signals on the list the nurse had given him, such as screaming and delirium. "So... here you are."

"You guys stayed up all night?" Billy asked.

94

"Took turns," Frank said.

"And you haven't gone to work," Billy said to Harold.

"I called in sick," he said with a grin.

"I really think you guys are wonderful. I just hate being so much trouble."

"Billy, would you do the same for one of us?" Frank asked.

"Of course."

"Then it's no trouble."

"Frank's right," Harold said.

Billy sat silent for a while, his feelings very mixed. To cover his confusion he asked, "How did you find me? Who would ever look for me in a dark alley at that hour?"

"Guess you don't remember that, either," Harold said. "You came stumbling down California Street, falling against the windows of the bar. Frank saw you. He looked up and you were kind of trying to walk while you were leaning against the windows."

"I didn't *break* one of those huge things, did I?"

"No," Frank said. "They're plate glass. You just rattled them a little. Good thing, too; might not have seen you."

"I guess. And the hospital must have cost money. My wallet's in my pants... isn't it?"

"Yeah," Harold said. "They didn't rob you. But just relax for now. We'll take care of all that later."

"Well... I am a little fuzzy-headed, have to admit," Billy said.

"Best thing right now," Frank said, "is just to take it easy. You can work out the details later. Listen, I have to go. Great to see you awake and all."

"Good seeing you again, Frank, and thanks."

"Sure."

Harold left the room with Frank and reurned a short time later. He found Billy sitting on the edge of the bed.

"You okay?"

"Trying to get to the bathroom, but I'm a little dizzy."

"Yeah. Probably all the painkiller and stuff they gave you. Let me help." With that he took a hold of Billy under his shoulders and brought him to his feet. Steadying the wavering body, Harold supported Billy almost completely as they walked across the room to the bathroom.

As Harold lowered him to the seat Billy groaned with pain, then tried to make light of it by commenting on what he discovered he was wearing: "You put me in a pair of your pajama bottoms." He grinned as best he could.

"Yeah. All I had. A little big. I left off the top because I thought it might irritate, or pull at your bandages. So, I'll be in the bedroom. Just yell when you need to get back to the bed." With that Harold closed the door and left Billy alone.

Harold sat in a chair and for the first time in twelve hours sensed his fatigue. He knew he was near exhaustion, but he did not feel sleepy. He was happy to see that Billy seemed to be talking and functioning pretty well, considering what he'd been through. No concussion, it looked like, and that was a relief after the night before, when Billy had had a brief bout of chills that ceased when Harold dressed the thin body in a pair of his pajama bottoms.

The worst was over, Harold knew, but he couldn't sleep. Billy's presence had brought up a whole scrapbook of memories, good and bad, that would not go away and let him rest. He figured that sooner or later this day he would just cave in.

The bathroom door opened, and Billy stood there. Harold leaped to his feet.

"No, let me try, I feel better, a little." Taking a few shaky steps, Billy managed to reach the bed. He settled in, Harold helping with the blankets. "Wow, I feel really pooped."

"You want to nap a while?"

"Yeah, I think I have to. But I want to tell you, I want to say I'll get out of here as soon as I can, and I'll—"

"We'll talk later, Billy. You want anything, just yell. I'll be out in the living room."

Frank lay in his bed trying to sleep. All the shades were pulled in his bedroom to keep out the afternoon light. He knew he had a shift to get through that evening, but he couldn't stop thinking about Harold having Billy back in his life. Nothing seemed different, true, but Frank felt that the situation was very dangerous for his relationship with Hal. He would do whatever he could to keep it going. . . .

Billy woke up late in the afternoon. Harold cooked them both a light meal. As they ate in the bedroom, Billy propped up against pillows in the bed, Harold in a chair, Billy asked, "Did you get any sleep?"

"Yeah, took quite a long snooze on the couch, woke up just before you did. . . . There's something I have to tell you, by the way. Frank and me? We're more than just friends."

Billy pretended to be surprised and said he was glad. He thought highly of Frank, and he knew how many worthless men there were in the city, men who might take advantage of Hal. "Frank's a great guy," Billy said.

"Yeah, he is."

Deek Jameson had checked everyone he knew for information about Billy. Using his connections, he discovered that there was a police report on Billy, indicating that he had been mugged the night before, had gotten treatment in a hospital emergency room, then had been released.

Now, on Tuesday evening, Deek was frantic. Quentin would never give up Nelson without getting Billy in trade. Quentin would find it all very amusing, a golden opportunity to indulge in a lot of teasing. And Jameson had his heart set on getting Nelson. Lately his fantasy life had been dominated by the image of Nelson — in leather, a jockstrap and running shoes, in nothing at all but with a whip in his hand.

Billy had to be found before Saturday — found and taken to Quentin's yacht. Deek didn't know how he would manage this, but when he became as single-minded as this, he usually got results, because he became implacable. This quirk of personality had gotten him to the top in business. Even now, all very discreetly, a detective agency was checking out the hotels in the Tenderloin and around the Polk area.

Finding Billy would probably cost a lot of money, and convincing him to visit Quentin on the yacht might require a fairly sizable cash gift. But that wasn't important to Deek. Having what he wanted was everything. And he knew, never having been beautiful himself, that what he wanted would not come to him. He always had to go out and grab it.

Later that same night, near last call, Frank looked up to see Harold coming into the bar.

"Hi, Hal. How's the kid?"

"He's asleep. I can't stay, in case he wakes up sick or something. He had a little bit of fever before he went to sleep. I don't think it's anything, but I better get back."

"Right," Frank said, feeling very down and trying not to show it. He sensed that he was losing Hal.

'I was just thinking, Frank, that maybe you could come over after vou finish here. We could use the couch."

Frank's mood brightened in an instant. "Sounds good to me. About two-thirty."

Harold nodded as he looked deep into Frank's eyes. Then he winked and left.

Watching Harold leave, Frank mixed a drink order and felt happy for the first time since Billy had come back on the scene.

Harold did not want to leave the bar, but he felt obliged to return to the apartment, to keep an eye out on Billy. Frank and the Beacon were good times, friendship, laughs, sexual pleasures. Billy and the apartment brought up memories of loneliness, turmoil, pain, his disgusting bouts of self-sorry drunkenness. Yes, and a certain amount of sexiness. He knew it couldn't be helped. Billy was young and beautiful, they had enjoyed some fine moments during their time together, and not all the memories were ugly.

Frank was the antidote for Billy and the past, Frank's hard, insistent body, strong and forceful tongue, his expert hands, his vast knowledge of the world of physical love.

Harold liked the fact that he always knew where he was at with Frank. That had not been the case with Billy, though now Harold knew that Billy had been confused himself and had meant no harm. Harold had liked it a lot when Frank and he were talking about their life as lovers, and Frank had said, "Any relationship between two men can be very simple. They set up their own personal rules, whatever suits them, and they stay strictly to them. That's all.... Being behind a bar, I see a lot of lovers slipping and sliding on each other. Why do they bother to be lovers? I just can't see it. It's so easy to work out something fitting, right? We going to be one to one, or do you want to be free to mess around a little on the side?"

Harold had been shocked, but hid it and calmly said, "I'm a one-man man, and you're the man."

"That's the way I feel too," Frank had said. "And if either one of us gets to feeling different about it, we don't sneak around, we talk, right?"

"Right," Harold had said, sure he would never want anyone but Frank, and happy with the sense of security he felt.

Billy woke Wednesday morning to find that Harold had gone off to work, leaving a note on the night table:

> Dear Billy — If you're not up to cooking breakfast, Frank will do it. Call him at home after eleven. He'll be up by then.
>
> Hal

Washing and shaving were slow processes for Billy, but he managed them. Making some toast, coffee, and fried eggs for himself was relatively easy. As he sat eating Billy decided he should move out as soon as possible. His black eye looked terrible, true, and his aches and pains still kept him from sleeping unless he took painkillers. The world outside was frightening and lonely, and the longer he stayed here, he knew, the harder it would be to become independent, to get on his own two feet. In a way, Harold was almost too kind. And there was another reason: Harold had Frank, and though they had given no indications at all, Billy was sure he was getting in the way of their life together.

Glumly he figured out how much money he had in the bank — not a lot — thought about finding some kind of job, and sadly considered which cheap hotel in the Tenderloin would be the least unpleasant place to rent a room.

The buzzer sounded for the door downstairs. Billy hobbled into the front hall as fast as his aches and pains and bandages would allow and pushed the button that would let the caller in. He waited at the apartment door, wondering if Hal was making a quick trip home from work at lunch hour. "Maybe he forgot his keys," Billy said to himself. He opened the door when he heard the elevator come to a stop and looked down the hall.

"Hi, Billy. Did I wake you?"

"Frank, hi. No. Come on in."

Frank followed Billy's slow journey to the kitchen and accepted a cup of coffee and a seat opposite him at the table. "Hal asked me to look in and see if you needed anything done for you. Or groceries or anything. Here, I brought today's paper."

"Thanks. No, I guess there's nothing. I can manage now, just a little slow and clumsy."

"Great. That shiner is healing fast. You can always tell a black eye's getting better when the bruises turn about eight different colors."

"Yeah," Billy said. "It's really a beaut."

"Swelling's all down in your face, though."

"Yes, a lot, and I'm really glad, because I'll be leaving tomorrow and start job hunting on Monday."

"Tomorrow?" Frank asked. "Isn't that a little soon?"

"I want to get settled in a room and... you know, get my life together."

"I can understand that. What's your plan?"

"Well, a room in the Tenderloin, some kind of job, busboy or dishwashing or anything I can find."

"What about college?"

"Well, maybe in January, I don't know."

Frank was surprised. From all he had heard, he'd figured Billy would go back to hustling rich guys, and he had thought that the kid would sponge off Harold's generosity until he connected with another wealthy old queen. But now, everything was changed. Maybe Billy was lying, but Frank doubted it very much. If the kid was going to go anyway, there'd be no harm in helping him on his way. Bunged up as he was right now, Billy was nothing but gorgeous, not to mention twenty years or so younger than Frank. So Billy wasn't a hustler, he was a good guy. Nice to know. But still, the sooner he was out of here the better....

"I know a couple of people who might be hiring," Frank said. "Start as busboy, keep your eyes open, become a waiter. It's good money and short hours. You can go to school with no problem, maybe as soon as January, I don't know."

"That'd be great."

"Have a piece of paper?"

"Uh... here." Billy pushed a long envelope across the table to Frank. "I was figuring my money on it," he said.

Frank wrote down some names and addresses. "I don't know the phone numbers, just look up these restaurants in the book."

"Thanks."

"Use my name. It might help."

"Great. Oh, uh... Hal told me about you two, and I just want to say I think it's really nice."

"I'm glad there's no hard feelings. Hey, you know there are some cheap hotels around Polk Street, workingmen's places they used to be, now mostly gay. Nothing fancy but not so dangerous as the Tenderloin to live in. You want some names?"

"Sure," Billy said, pushing the envelope back to Frank, who began to write on it.

After a short time Frank looked up at Billy. "I couldn't help but see your figures here. That all the money you have?"

"Well... yes."

"Won't last you a week."

"The job I had, I sent a lot of money home to my mother, she lost her job when the steakhouse closed. Kind of rough for a while, but she's doing fine now, wants to pay me back as soon as she can. That'll help... when it comes."

"Yeah. . . . Look, here's a hundred bucks. No, no, don't be noble and start objecting. It's a loan. I'll put it inside the envelope. Pay me back when you get on your feet, okay?"

"Frank, that's too generous. I can't."

"With the cash you have right now, Billy, you'll only last a few days. If you don't get a job, if you do get one but will have to wait a week or two weeks or maybe longer to get paid, then what? Some old fart'll offer you a few bucks to put out, and you'll be hungry, maybe owing rent, and — well, just take the loan, okay?"

"Well. . . All right, I will," Billy said. He was determined to get a job Monday and not spend a penny of the loan, but it would be good to have the money just in case.

Billy felt much happier for Frank's visit. The world outside didn't appear nearly so terrifying now.

Frank left the apartment building and headed to the athletic club for a swim. He did not feel too proud of himself, but he was glad that Billy wasn't a hustler after all. The kid might even pay me back, he thought. Better the way it turned out than what I had planned.

What Frank had planned was to pay Billy to leave town, at a bargain rate he had hoped; but, having some knowledge of hustlers, he had brought along a total of five hundred dollars.

Suddenly a notion flashed into Frank's mind: If Billy wasn't hustling Deek, maybe he loved him. But something must have happened. After we had him out of the emergency room and Hal asked him if he wanted to go back to Jameson's, he practically got hysterical, said he couldn't go back there. And I thought Jameson was tired of him and threw him out. Odd, all of it, but it's good to know the kid's not a whore. . . .

In the evening when Harold came home, Billy phoned for a pizza. He wanted to show his appreciation some way, but cooking a whole dinner was too difficult, and he thought it might look too domestic, as if he were trying to remind Hal of the old days.

After they finished eating, Billy told Harold that he would be leaving in the morning. Harold protested that it was too soon, but Billy remained firm. "I'll be fine."

"You have enough money?"

"Plenty, Hal. No problem. I'm okay, really."

"Well. . . ."

"And. . . just let me say a couple of things that I've had on my mind for a while. Um, like, that scene with Deek. You were right. He was using me. I couldn't see it at all, then, but it was true. And something else. About us. I should have tried harder, I know that. And the strange thing is that every stupid thing I did seemed to be the right thing to do at the time. I guess it all comes down to what I really want to say: I never tried to hurt you on purpose, and I never *wanted* to hurt you. With all the dumb shit that I did I guess that's hard to believe, but it's true, and I want you to know it."

Harold sat very quietly, saying nothing, for some long moment of time. "I knew that, Billy, but I'm glad you told me. And, what the hell, I wasn't perfect. A lot of my problem was that the city scared me. And you were right, I didn't let you stand on your own feet."

The silence thickened so much that they were both about to drown in it. Finally Billy managed to say, "Oh, Frank came by to see if he could help me out, and we talked a little bit."

"Yeah? I thought he would."

"And every time he said your name, I could hear a kind of special sound in his voice. He really loves you, Hal."

Now Billy felt safe from the troublesome feelings raised by the conversaion.

He went on: "I told him I knew about you two and thought it was great."

Later that same Thursday evening, Warren came into the Beacon bar for a few drinks and a visit with Frank. "Harold coming in?" he asked. "Or has he already been?"

"I don't think he'll be in," Frank replied. "The kid is still kind of sickly. But he's leaving tomorrow."

"So you and Harold can get it on again?"

"Oh, we've been managing. Ball on the couch, which by the way, is where Hal has been sleeping."

"And blondie shut away in the bedroom? Lovely idea."

"Why Warren," Frank said, a teasing glint in his eye, "you sound worried about our relationship. Aren't they all doomed from the start?"

"All rules have exceptions, they say. Besides, I have a kind of proprietary interest. You and Mr. Biceps happened before my very eyes, here in the bar and then at that party. You two make a nice couple, so I don't want anything bad to happen, that's all."

"Aha, we bring out the fairy godmother in you, pardon the expression."

"Why not? You know I'd love to prove myself wrong. And frankly, when we lugged that kid into my car the other night, Harold had quite an expression on his face."

"Just pity," Frank said. "You have to admit the kid did look pretty pathetic, blood all over his face and clothes, mud in his hair, all that. And like I said, Billy's leaving tomorrow."

Harold woke with a start, then sat up on the couch in Frank's apartment where he had been dozing for some hours. The metallic clanks and clicks that had awakened him ceased as Frank came in the door.

"Hal!"

"Hi, Frank."

The two men met in a big hug and kiss.

Harold said, "I let myself in, hope you don't mind."

"No, of course not. That's why I gave you a set of keys. Something up?"

"No. Just... restless, I guess. Billy's sleeping, went to bed early, so I came over here.... I thought that maybe, if you're not too tired from work, we could—"

"Get it on?" Frank asked with a smile.

"Or just sleep, long as we're together."

"Let's get it on first, then sleep together."

"Sounds good to me," Harold said.

"And we even can mess around in a bed, for a change, how about that? Come on, let's go to the bedroom."

As they undressed Frank said, "You going to bring me my dinner tomorrow night, or should I pack a lunch?"

"I'll buy it. What do you want?"

"A burrito from Garcia's deli? Hot sauce si, onions no?"

"Okay," Harold said.

In a short time the bedroom was illuminated only by one weak bulb that cast a diffuse light over the two naked male bodies on the creaking bed. The big man, lying face down under the little man, was moaning "Harder... harder... harder...."

11

Harold returned to his own apartment very early in the morning. He knew he would be tired at work, but he had slept at Frank's, some before Frank got home and a little afterwards. A quick shower, a change of clothes, some breakfast, and he'd be ready to face the job. And tomorrow was Saturday; he could sleep late.

Early as it was, he found Billy up and dressed.

"I thought you'd be asleep," Harold said.

"Woke up early. What I get for crapping out at eight o'clock last night. I was just waiting to say goodbye... and to thank you."

"So early? Let's have breakfast at least."

"Well... okay. Look, I can cook it if you want to get ready."

"All right," Harold said. "I'll take my shower and change."

After breakfast, which they ate while listening to the day's news on the radio, Billy said, "Well, now it really is time to go." He got up from the table.

"Well, if you really feel you're up to it," Harold said. "Might be a good idea to at least stay the weekend." He followed Billy into the living room.

"I better get my life going again," Billy said. "Thanks, though."

"You need money?" Harold asked. They were at the door.

"No, I'm okay, Hal." Billy put his hand on the knob and opened the door. He smiled at Harold and stepped into the hall. As he turned to go toward the elevator, a hand took hold of his shoulder.

"Billy?"

The young man turned around and faced Harold. "Yes?"

"Walk you to the elevator," Harold said gruffly.

Billy nodded and they went down the hall to the metal door. Billy punched the button. From far below their feet came the muffled thudding rattles of the machinery getting into motion.

They stood side by side in silence, neither able to think of anything to say. The little square of window in the door suddenly turned yellow with light, and a loud click sounded from the innards of the door itself. Billy pulled it open.

He stepped forward and was embraced from behind. He was drawn back into the hallway. "Hal, don't. Please." The elevator door swung shut.

"I still love you. I tried to forget you, to stop loving you, but I can't."

"Hal, let me go."

At once the powerful arms rose away from Billy, who turned around to face Harold. "I still love you, too. I knew it the moment you touched me, when you were helping me into the bathroom. Your feel, your strength, your smell, they all did it to me. . . . But it's too late. Hal, I really tried to be a straight shooter this time. You're the one making it hard for us." With that, Billy turned around again and opened the elevator door. He pushed aside the folding metal grating and stepped inside the little chamber.

"It's not too late, Billy, if we love each other."

Billy looked at Harold through the metal strips of the grating. "Sure it is, Hal. You've got Frank."

"Billy! Goddammit!"

"Let go the door, Hal. Don't make it any harder than it is." At that point Billy's exhaustion was complete. He had no more will, no more pretense, nothing. He turned away, desperately trying to control himself, to keep the tears from showing. "Close the goddamned door!" he roared over his shoulder.

105

He heard a rattle and waited for the car to begin its downward motion. Then he could open his eyes and turn around.

Two big hands pulled Billy from his corner, picked him up and carried him out of the elevator.

Billy looked up and saw Harold's face streaming tears.

"We're lovers!" Harold groaned. "You son of a bitch, don't you see that? You and me! Not Frank, not anyone! Us!"

Billy reached up his arms and joined them around Harold's sturdy neck, then he pulled himself tight against the man who was holding him.

"Don't cry," Billy whispered, choking as he tried to stop his own tears. Don't cry, lover."

"I . . . I'm okay now," Harold said. He moved on up the hall, carrying Billy in his arms. "I'm taking you home, darling . . . if you'll let me."

"Take me home," Billy said. "Please take me home."

In a few moments an apartment door, given a sharp kick, slammed shut. Then, several minutes after that the elevator shaft sounded with thuds and clanks again. The window in the metal door lost its yellow glow, which sank down and out of sight, to be replaced by a dull grey color.

That afternoon, as they lunched in an elegant downtown restaurant full of ferns and palms, Quentin said to Deek, "But my dear, I had my heart set on Billy. And if you can't provide him for me, I'm afraid that Nelson is out of the question."

"What nonsense," Deek snapped. "Billies are a dime a dozen."

"Dearest, I'll put up the dime, you find me even one pliant young man who is as incredibly gorgeous as that Billy. As for Nelson, he's keeping watch on my yacht, which is located somewhere in the Bay Area, but not, I guarantee you, at the San Francisco marina. I know you'd simply go and buy him away from me, if you could find him."

"There's more than one Nelson around, too," Deek said.

"Very few hustlers have his skills or his enthusiasm for . . . whatever it is you like to do in your blackroom."

"Really, Quentin, we're supposed to be friends, and you are taking every advantage of this misfortune. Sometmes I think you carry your own peculiar brand of sadism too far."

"Ah, Deek, such accusations But why worry? You have until Saturday morning to find him and it's now only Thursday afternoon. . . ."

106

Harold had arrived at work just on time, and the place was very busy. But all day long he hummed to himself and wore a little smile on his face. And every so often he would take in a sharp breath through his nose.

Over and over he recalled the events of the morning, especially those that took place when he brought Billy back into the apartment in his arms and lay him on the bed. They had pulled themselves together, lying in each other's arms very lightly, so as not to touch any of Billy's painful areas, and then Harold had said, softly into Billy's ear, "Let me suck your cock before I go to work."

"Why, Hal," Billy said, surprised.

Harold grinned down on his lover's bruised, black-eyed face. "Not so uptight as I used to be. Let me suck you off. I *have* to go to work, missed too many days lately, but — please."

"Oh, yes, darling, do it."

Carefully, so as not to jostle Billy, Harold undid the buttons of his lover's jeans, and pulled them down just enough to bring cock and balls into view. Maneuvering delicately, he swung himself between Billy's legs. "Just lie back, lover," he said softly. Then he licked his way from the inner thighs to the pubic hair, and traced the length of Billy's hardening cock with his tongue, up to the tip and around the head and down to the balls, tight-held in highly contracted scrotal flesh. They proved very sensitive.

When Harold felt his beloved was sufficiently aroused, he set to work, taking the cock deeper and deeper into his powerful, busy mouth. The first time he throated the cock, Billy's body hardened with the thrill that ran all through it. On the second time he felt two smooth young hands grip his shoulders. "Hal, I, oh I'm... ohhhh!"

Billy's groan of ecstasy repeated itself in Harold's mind all day long. And he had not drunk all Billy's semen. He'd let some of it dry on his moustache. As he worked he fancied he could smell it if he breathed in through his nose fast and hard. From time to time, when nobody was looking, he quickly licked his facial hair with his tongue.

"I could go get you some food," Warren said to Frank that evening in the Beacon. "You're eating every peanut in the bar."

"Thanks, but Hal will be showing up with the burrito any minute now... guess he dozed off. Sometimes he comes home from that job really bushed."

"Okay, suffer if you want, " Warren said. "By the way, did you hear that Arthur Charles fell and broke his ankle?"

"Yeah?"

"During his show last night. Must have had a loose hem on one of his gowns. I think he's up at St. Joseph's."

"I'll buy a big get-well card, pass it around the bar, have the regulars sign it."

"Sounds like a nice idea," Warren said.

Frank went off to attend some of the other customers, and he had his back to the door when Harold came in, burrito in hand.

"Hi, Frank."

The bartender turned around. "Hal, at last.... Mmm, the burrito feels nice and hot. Thanks. Want a beer?"

"Uh, no. Gotta go. When you have a minute could we talk for a little?"

"Sure," Frank said. He finished the drinks he was making, checked to see that his customers were happy, then went down to the end of the bar where Harold had taken a seat.

"Well, what's up, Hal?"

"I just came over to, well, bring your dinner, and sorry I'm late with it, but I have to tell you something too: Billy and I, uh Billy and I — he didn't leave this morning."

Warren, a few seats off, couldn't hear what was being said, but he sensed that the matter was serious, judging by the expression on Harold's face and by the intense way that Frank was leaning over the bar toward him.

"You two back together?" Frank asked, in a neutral, quiet voice.

"Right. Yes. We are."

Warren thought Harold looked slightly comic, being so big and right now so very nervous. Frank, on the other hand, appeared calm. His face had become mask-like, expressionless, without any emotion at all.

"Well," Frank said, "so you're back with Billy. That's good. You two belong together."

"We do," Harold said. "It's true.... I'm glad you understand it the way you do."

"Just the way things go," Frank said. "No problem."

Warren watched his friend talking and saw a little smile form on his face. It wasn't exactly forced, it was the grin of someone without further resources. Warren made a good guess about the subject matter. That cheap hustling blond trash had his hooks back into Harold, handy guy to sponge off of, until he could score another millionaire. Dumping a great guy like Frank for that pretty little tart, Warren

108

thought. Boy, is that jerk Harold going to be sorry, and it'll serve him right.

Down the bar the two men faced each other in silence.

Finally Harold said, "Frank, we like the bar, and we like you, but if you'd rather we didn't come in here any more, well, we understand."

"Come on, Hal. We're all grownups. No harm's intended, right? Don't worry about it. You and Billy come in any time you want."

Harold smiled for the first time since he had come into the Beacon. He said, "Well, I gotta be getting back." He took Frank's two hands in his own, gave them a squeeze, then left the bar as fast as he could without actually running.

Outside Harold breathed deep, realizing he had been almost holding his breath while in the bar. He felt extremely relieved. Frank had been great about it. No way had seemed right — trying to get home from work in time to see Frank before he went to work at six, waiting to tell Frank when he returned to his apartment at two-thirty or three in the morning, going to the bar to tell him while he was working. . . .

After Harold had eaten the dinner that Billy cooked, and while they were wrestling around on the couch together, still clothed but with sex very much in mind, Harold had remembered that Frank expected him to bring a burrito for dinner. He had gone into the bar in a state of near-panic. Of all the people in the world to hurt, Frank was his last choice.

Now it was all over. Now he could return to Billy feeling good. This morning when he left Frank's bed he never thought it would be for the last time. So much had happened since. His life with Frank now seemed to be something remembered from long ago.

Inside the bar Warren watched Frank, still leaning on his elbows, looking down, not moving.

"Bartender!" came from far up the bar.

As Warren observed, Frank picked up a set of keys that Harold had silently left behind and put them in his pocket. Warren began to nurse his drinks, ask for light shots in them, because he felt somebody should stay with Frank. Warren wanted to do more but could think of nothing, especially when Frank was so insistent on keeping it all to himself. But Warren knew him well, could see the nervous edge to his movements, his heightened concentration on his work and increased speed. And Warren saw the burrito sitting on the bar-back, ignored or forgotten.

After most of the neighborhood regulars had cleared out, and the bar was heading for closing with only a few diehards scattered here and there, Frank and Warren were able to talk.

"You're sure as hell staying out late tonight," Frank said.

"I'm all nervous and wide awake," Warren said. "Can I buy the bartender a drink?"

"Oh, I don't think that — well, what the hell. A good gin and tonic might be nice. Thanks." With that, Frank poured a very stiff drink, as Warren happened to notice. He made another drink for Warren, too.

"Chin-chin and all that rot," Frank said, and they toasted and drank. "Guess what?"

"What, Frank?"

"Hal has gone back to Billy."

"Oh?"

"All very sudden. Real gent about it, came in and told me up front and looking right in my eyes."

"I saw him come in," Warren said.

"That's when he did it. Oh well. I don't know, maybe you're right about gay relationships, Warren. Maybe I shouldn't even try to have a long-term lover until we're both in our nineties. We can hold hands in the old folks' home, and the biggest thrill will be when the attendant gives us our baths. Except of course that whoever I choose would probably like somebody else's hand better than mine after a while, a short while. 'Sorry, Frank, but Herby's liver spots are wilder than yours, so adios, baby.' Something like that. Hey, I'm bending your ear. Now you tell me about your day."

"Come on, Frank. We're friends. You want to talk? Well, talk."

"Me talk? Me manic? Me about to explode? What nonsense, my dear. You know Hal and I fucked today, almost till dawn? So this, tonight, came as kind of a surprise. Ah, I should have known when he was late with my burrito."

Warren couldn't help but laugh, and he liked the fact that Frank was laughing a little too.

Frank went on: "Well, so much for this morning. Take my yesterday. Please! For instance, I did happen to lend Billy a hundred bucks so he could go off and start a new life. I must congratulate myself for having the wit to think that there was a certain amount of danger, to me and Hal that is, in having those two ex-lovers in the same apartment together. So you can't call me a complete fool, man. I did sense their vibes with each other. I thought they were just leftovers, or I hoped they were. . . . Hoo haa. I even gave Billy a list of cheap but decent hotels and some job leads. . . ."

Frank fell silent, seeming to have run out of steam. Warren felt helpless seeing his friend's suffering, knowing the external silliness was a cover for real misery within. He also loathed Billy, seeing him as a coldhearted, heedless young man, selfishly messing up lives as he traded on his good looks in the higher reaches of prostitution. How many times he had seen this pattern before. . . .

"Last call," Frank said.

By two a.m. Billy and Harold had been asleep for hours. Billy had waited for his lover to return from the Beacon, fearing Hal would be in a terrible mood as a result of Frank's reaction. But Harold came in happy and relaxed, all praise for Frank.

In a short time they were naked together on their bed, making love. Because of Billy's bruises they went slowly, richly prolonging every lick and stroke, and a mutual carefulness passed into a precise intensity of action. Silently, diligently, each man loved the other to the limit of his ability. For both it seemed that their sensual awareness had immensely increased, that they had somehow gotten beyond hangups and limitations, had burst into a world of limitless sensual pleasure. Neither man realized just how much he had learned about loving in the past few months. Each thought he was just experiencing a deluge of stored-up passion for the other.

Billy ran his hand up Harold's hard inner thigh as he pressed his lover back to the pillow with a deep kiss. Feeling the fuzz of the leg give way to thick, damp, pubic curls, Billy slid his hand down under the hot, sweaty balls and found the hard bulge of the base of his lover's cock. He pressed it and kneaded it firmly, tonguing Hal's nipples all the while. As he worked, Billy had to fight against the pair of thighs that held his wrist, limiting the movements of his exploring hand, until their pressure melted away. Thus freed, Billy dug deeper, reaching one finger into a warmth of flesh to touch the skin where it became a rough-surfaced oval.

In the back of Billy's mind came the thought that Hal had never allowed anything like this before, but Billy had no fear. Everything they were doing was so exactly right, they could do nothing wrong.

Quickly finding the lubricant lying beside one of the pillows, Billy slowly moved his slippery finger into Harold. At once the big thighs clamped against Billy's lower arm, and then relaxed again.

Never stopping his rhythmic explorations with his finger, Billy arranged himself in a kneeling position between Harold's legs, which forced them to open wider. He bent forward and took his lover's hard cock in his mouth.

In a short time Harold was groaning and sighing, and when Billy felt his lover was close to coming he turned him over onto his belly, applied some lubricant to himself, rose up over Harold's magnificently muscled body, and sank into him.

They found they hardly dared move, so close were they to ejaculation. But they could not lie still for long, and Billy's thrusting rhythms grew from mere tics to long, deep-going arcs. His moves were answered by Harold raising his haunches to take each stroke to its furthest limit. They moved as one, faster and faster, until they could not stop themselves or turn back or slow down. Harold clung to the mattress in order not only to bear the pain but also to try to keep from thrashing about too much and hurting his still-bandaged lover. Billy clung for dear life to Harold's massive back. As they joined again and again, harder and faster, the golden ache spread all through them from its birthplace deep in the heat of their loins. It turned to pure ecstasy for an endless instant of time. They let forth groans of futile but delicious resistance and the blazing liquids exploded from their writhing, pounding bodies.

In a little while, sweaty, slick with ejaculate, greasy here and there with lubricant, they lay in each other's arms, breathing hard, noisily, and deeply. When they could talk they said nothing, just gazed at each other, smiled and kissed until their afterglow faded into sleep.

Alone in his apartment, Frank sat in the living room and smoked a joint. It was his third so far. He hoped sleep would come with this one. The television was going. He had watched the Late Night Movie, the Red Eye Movie Club, and now the Sunrise Cinema program had begun. Vaguely he remembered Jean Harlow talking with Marie Dressler, Audie Murphy fighting a war, and an Italian film with obscure actors, something about spies in a posh ski resort. Now several of the Lane Sisters were staring blank-eyed at each other and talking cute inanities.

Frank sucked deep on the joint, again and again until it was a tiny, unmanageable stub. Then, determined to sleep, he let his clothes drop to the floor, fetched a blanket, and lay back on the couch. The television's light, all there was in the room, held his eye, but his mind was far away. Hal. Hal. Hal. . . . Hal whose faint odor remained in the sheets on the bed, whose picture sat on the chest of drawers. . . .

Frank idly wondered how he would get through the hectic Friday night shift he faced in relatively few hours. He knew he would not have time to swim or do anything, not that there was a thing in the world that seemed worth doing. And he knew that what had happened was for the best. Those two had never stopped loving each other, not really. And Frank knew too that he had tried too hard, used his skills to give Harold the illusion of love. It was the real thing only for me, he thought. . . .

12

On Friday morning Harold got ready for work while Billy prepared breakfast, As they were having a last cup of coffee Billy said, "This is my plan: I'll clean up the apartment and do the laundry today. Then, on Monday I'll find a job. It's too late to start school, but I can sign up for it in January, and maybe by then I'll have a little money ahead."

"You don't need to worry about a job," Harold said.

"I want a job. And by the way, Hal, your housekeeping really went to hell while I was gone. Were you all that busy?"

"No. I just didn't care very much.... Look, can we make a deal? Let's not talk about the time when we were apart, okay?"

"I didn't mean anything," Billy said, speaking now with great seriousness.

"Billy, I know. It's just. .. I don't know how to explain it."

"I think I understand, Hal. There s not much about it I want to remember anyway, myself.... If you had Frank for a lover, well, I think you were a lot better off than I was. Okay, it's a deal."

"Good."

"And listen, Billy: I know the place is kind of a mess, but I'll help you clean it up tomorrow, and Sunday too, if it takes that long."

"Hal, I was exaggerating," Billy said. "It'll be easy to get everything cleaned up today. Then you and I can have the whole weekend to play."

"Okay," Hal said. "We'll go to any bar you want. It's too bad that Arthur Charles guy broke his — never mind."

"Whoops," Billy said. "I know we're not going to talk about that time, but did you see me there, at the night club?"

"Yeah."

"Subject closed," Billy said. "Well... he *is* very funny. Maybe when he does another show you and I can go and enjoy him... maybe that'll take the curse off. Or if you'd rather not...."

"I think we already got the curse off us," Harold said. "I just didn't want you to think we're always just going to stay home. No use getting bored."

"Oh, I see. Well, my idea for this weekend was in fact to sort of stay home... maybe even spend a lot of time in bed. Maybe pop into the Beacon for a couple of beers. Then, next weekend... well, whatever you like."

"Sounds like a good idea to me, Billy. We'll take the weekends as they come...."

Harold and Billy left the apartment a short time later, Billy with a big sack of laundry on his shoulder. They parted only when the bus came along. Billy waved goodbye and walked on down the street to the laundromat.

Frank woke up late and he felt groggy. But the worst of his pain was over, and he was thankful for that. Some grey days lay ahead, he knew, but he felt capable of dealing with life if not exactly eager to do so.

He got up, made a pot of coffee and drank five cups of it. As he showered he remembered he had to buy a card for Arthur Charles before he went to work.

Returning from the laundromat, Billy worked hard around the apartment until he finished cleaning it up, in mid-afternoon. As he rested a sudden thought came. Yes, he had to do something very disagreeable. There was no way around it, except by making a large sacrifice, which Billy was extremely unwilling to do. Might as well get it over with, he told himself.

Billy picked up the phone and dialed. "Mr. Jameson, please....
Oh, uh, just say it's Billy.... Deek? This is Billy.... Yes, I'm fine. I,
uh, left a few things at your place, and I'd like to pick them up. If
you'd send them down to the doorman, just the stuff I brought, my
little suitcase, like that, I'd appreciate it.... Oh, great. When could
I—? Fine. Let's see, it's almost four. I'll be there at four-thirty.... Oh,
no, you don't need to send the car.... Oh, with my stuff in it. Well,
that's very kind. I'll wait for it downstairs in front of my building."
Billy gave the address to Jameson. After they hung up he quickly
washed off the housecleaning dirt, changed into clean clothes, and
went down to the entrance of the apartment building.

The big black car arrived in a short time, and the chauffeur said he
was sorry but that Billy's clothes had been misplaced, and would he
come up to the apartment and discuss the matter with Mr. Jameson?

Billy wanted to be at home when Hal arrived from work, in about
an hour. Jameson's place wasn't far away. "Well, okay," he said, and
got into the limousine.

Warren usually returned home from his job in the financial district via
the Sacramento Street trolley, but today, as on most Fridays, he had a
leisurely after-work drink with a few friends in a gay bar off Montgomery Street, then treated himself to a leisurely, scenic ride home on
the California Street cable car.

He suspected he was the lone San Franciscan among the mass of
chattering, pointing, camera-laden tourists, and it was amusing to
watch their increasing nervousness as the little hundred-year-old car
moved steadily up the long, steep eastern slope of Nob Hill, drawn by
a single cable grinding along in a narrow slot in the pavement.

Warren's thoughts turned again to Frank. He had been thinking
about him all day at work. How to comfort his friend without getting
sticky or smothery or irritating — that was the problem that had been
occupying him since he'd gotten up this morning. Frank was easy to
communicate with when he was on top of it all, outgoing and lively,
but when something bad happened, Warren knew, his friend froze up,
went blank to the world. He felt that Frank sometimes was too private
a person, keeping all his hurt inside. Wish I knew what to do, Warren
thought.

The cable car reached the summit of Nob Hill, a plateau where
many of the passengers got off and headed for the Mark Hopkins or
the Fairmont or one of the other big hotels in the vicinity.

Then, passing the dark Gothic mass of Grace Cathedral on one side and the flatly modern white marble Masonic Auditorium on the other, the machine started down Nob Hill's gentle western slope.

A few blocks further, Warren stood up and called out his corner to the brakeman. When the car came to a stop Warren got off, and it rattled away, trailing the campfire odor of its pine-block brakes.

Making his way to the sidewalk through the busy afternoon traffic, Warren saw something startling: a limousine, headed up Nob Hill, back the way he had come, that held a chauffeur and that blond kid, Billy.

Warren reached the sidewalk feeling a great contempt for the passenger in the automobile. But this was more than balanced by a revival of hope for Frank's happiness with Harold.

"Billy," Jameson said. "Come in. Let's sit down in the living room, shall we?"

When they were settled, Jameson, charming as ever, said, "I'm afraid I was rather forgetful. The truth of the matter is that I sent your clothes over to Quentin Wales' house."

"What?"

"Well, he was terribly interested in you, and I thought you might enjoy being with him. But that's all in the past. I gather you have a life of your own now."

"Yes," Billy said, refusing to respond to Jameson's charm, now knowing it for what it really was. "All I really want is my old suitcase. Are you sure it's still not here?"

"Go and look if you like, " Jameson said. "But I am sure everything went over to Quentin's."

Billy kept himself from making any bitter remarks about being traded and used. "Yeah, I want to look," Billy said, not caring if Jameson liked his word doubted or not.

Coming back from the rooms that had until recently been his own, Billy said, "Empty, all right. What's Quentin's phone number?"

"Billy, I realize you are not happy in my company, though I honestly don't understand why you left me. And I understand how important it is for you to get your things back. So I called Quentin, and he says we should go to his house. Let me take you."

Billy didn't like the idea at all, suspicious that Jameson and Wales might try to talk him into being Quentin's playtoy. And Hal would be home pretty soon. . . . I can always call him and say I'm coming, he thought.

117

"Well, okay," Billy said.

In the limousine Jameson directed the chauffeur to take them to Quentin's house, which was far over in Pacific Heights.

During the ride Jameson asked Billy, "Tell me, why did you leave?"

"Personal reasons," Billy said, then gazed out the windows at the large homes and apartment houses that lined the streets, making it clear that he didn't want to say anything more.

Around five-thirty in the afternoon Harold arrived home, tired but happy. He found the apartment neat and clean but empty. He sat down to rest, expecting the return of his lover from the grocery store or wherever he had gone.

"Ah, Deek, Billy, good to see you both," Quentin boomed, meeting them at the door of his huge Victorian house and sweeping them through several rooms full of ornate antique furniture to a big, comfortable den. To Billy it looked like an ideal masculine interior, the kind of thing he'd seen before only in magazine advertisements for liquor or toiletries.

"Well, sit down, make yourselves comfortable," Quentin went on. "So, Deek tells me that you want to get your clothes and suitcase."

"Yes," Billy answered, wishing Quentin wouldn't stare at him that way. "He said they were here."

"They were here," Quentin said, "but they're not any more."

"Oh?"

"Billy, you see, I had plans for us, for you and me. I thought you and I might sail the South Seas together for a few months, just relax and enjoy life. So, with that in mind, I had your clothes taken out to the yacht."

"I see," Billy said, again unpleasantly reminded by Quentin's warm, friendly words of the cold-hearted conversation he had overheard not many nights before. "Well, I can go down to the marina, and if someone's on board, maybe they can give me my—"

"The craft is not at the local marina," Quentin said. "I had to have it fitted out and some repairs done, so it's over at the Berkeley marina."

"Berkeley?"

"But Billy," Jameson said, "we could be over there and back in an hour."

"An hour?" Billy asked, panicked. "Well... can I make a phone call?"

Quentin showed him to a telephone in one of the rooms full of dark, scrolly furnishings.

As Billy heard the rings come, one after another, he figured that an hour from now would be seven-thirty, so he could easily be back by eight.

After a dozen rings with no answer Billy put down the phone, thinking it best to give up, call his suitcase lost and let it go at that.

He went back into the den to say goodbye and Quentin said, "Ah, there you are. We're already to go, and the car's waiting."

"Okay," Billy said. He could always call from Berkeley.

At the Beacon the after-work crowd had thinned out, and the big Friday night crowd hadn't yet come in. Frank had seen Harold pass by the bar a couple of times, out on California Street, and now he saw the big guy come in.

He sat down, ordered a beer, and casually asked Frank, "You haven't seen Billy around, have you?"

"Billy? No, can't say I have."

"Thanks," Harold said. Then, much to Frank's puzzlement, his friend sauntered out smiling, saying a casual goodbye, and left behind him an almost untouched bottle of beer.

Frank wondered if Harold and Billy had gotten into a lovers' quarrel already. He felt good about one thing, that Harold's appearance wasn't too upsetting: Frank knew he still wanted Harold, but not in an overwhelming way, now. A shrugging indifference to Harold was a long way off, Frank was sure, but he sensed that he was back on his feet.

The ride across the bay bridge to Berkeley did indeed take only a half hour. Billy went aboard with Quentin and Deek. A young man greeted them. Billy thought him very handsome, with slightly thick features and a closely cut head of black hair. He noticed that Jameson was fascinated with the young man, who was introduced as Nelson.

To Billy's question Quentin answered, "Your stuff? Oh, it's in the cabin below. Right, Nelson?"

"Right, Quentin."

Billy rushed down to the little room, familiar and loaded with unpleasant memories. He found his suitcase and clothes neatly arranged in a small built-in closet. He opened the battered piece of luggage, was relieved to find its contents untouched, and filled it with a few items of clothing, stuff he had owned before he knew Jameson. He left everything else hanging in the closet.

He planned to call Hal from a pay phone, and try the Beacon if his lover wasn't at home, then get back to The City as fast as possible Now that night had settled in firmly, Billy wanted more than ever to be back home with Harold and never see these creeps.

As he lugged the suitcase upstairs, Billy felt unsteady. Suddenly realizing what must be happening, he bounded up the staircase at top speed, suitcase banging against the bulkhead as he went. Up on deck he saw Berkeley receding. Several hundred feet of dark water lay between the yacht and the shore.

"Stop! Go back! I've got to get home!"

Harold was frantic by eight in the evening. He checked everywhere he could think of in the neighborhood, laundromats, such stores as were still open, the Beacon, the streets. Then he went back to the apartment and prayed for the phone to ring. After nearly an hour of waiting and fighting off terrible thoughts, Harold went to check the one place he had avoided before, the nearby St. Francis Hospital.

Billy was not in the emergency room and not listed as a patient.

Harold went back to the apartment and began telephoning the many other hospitals in San Francisco. Between each call he would wait for some minutes, hoping the phone would ring.

Finally it did.

"Hello?"

"Hello! I'm Michael Smith, and I'm calling about the Sheriff's Rodeo, a benefit for—"

Harold slung the receiver onto its cradle. "Billy!" he cried. "Goddammit! Billy!"

"You tricked me!" Billy yelled at Jameson.

"It's a mixup!" Quentin roared. "I thought you understood. We're bringing Deek and Nelson back to The City. And we're having dinner on the way."

Realizing there was nothing he could do, and hoping Quentin was telling the truth about returning to The City, Billy turned away from the two older men in the wheelhouse, and made his way down the deck to the railing at the stern. He recalled the conversation he'd overheard: "...could come with me on the yacht... company on my cruise to the South Seas...." Billy concluded that Jameson and Wales had cooked all this up beween them. Wales is going to try to talk me into going with him, Billy thought, wishing he were a champion swimmer with super night vision and a waterproof suitcase.

Billy's anxiety increased when he noticed that the yacht was moving north in the bay, not west towards San Francisco. He wondered why they came to a halt in the cove of a high, dark island. Because it was getting colder, Billy opened his suitcase and put on a heavier jacket. The island showed no signs of life, no wires, no phone booths, not even any place to dock.

Quentin's voice came from the door of the deck level cabin: "Billy, you don't have to sulk all night. Come on in and have some dinner."

"I'm not hungry," Billy called back, then returned his gaze to the bright mound of lights that was San Francisco.

Half an hour later Billy heard the cabin door open and a figure approached the stern, walking with a desperate stagger. Laughter, loud and derisive, came from the cabin. The man, who Billy now realized was Nelson, suddenly veered off to the railing, as if suddenly discovering his intended goal.

Billy saw him lean over and heard him vomiting.

"Seasick!" came Quentin's shout. "On the bay! What a sailor... probably gets ill taking a bath!"

The laughter of two men followed

Billy, drawing closer to Nelson, saw that he seemed to be done with his vomiting and looked about to sink to the deck with weakness.

"Let me help you," Billy said.

Nelson groaned.

Billy got him below to the tiny room that contained a wash basin, then left him and returned to the stern.

By ten p.m. the Beacon was crowded and getting more so. Warren sat at his usual place around the back curve of the bar and observed Frank at work. He was surprised, knowing how Frank must feel, to see him joking and bantering as he made change and kept the drinks coming.

"Hi, Warren "

"Oh, Harold. How are you doing?"

"I'm looking for Billy. You haven't seen him around, have you?"

Warren looked into the worried face of the man who was standing over him. He felt sorry for Hal, felt he shouldn't be put through all this. "Well, Harold, I saw him this afternoon, when I was coming home from work."

"When?"

"About four-thirty, I guess. He was going up California Street, towards the top of Nob Hill in a car."

"A car?" Hal asked, puzzled.

"Well, a limousine, with a chauffeur in it."

Warren hated himself thoroughly when he saw Harold suddenly take on the look of a man who's been punched in the gut. But if Harold didn't know about that little blond hustler now, he might wait and wait for him. It could be weeks before he and Frank would get back together again.

"Uh, thanks," Harold mumbled, then left the bar almost as if sleep-walking.

"Howdy, stranger," Quentin said as he came up to Billy, who was startled from his preoccupations. "Brought you some food and a drink. Gin and tonic, think that's what you like...." Billy made no move to turn from the railing, so Quentin set the plate and glass on the deck. "You know," he went on, "we didn't mean any harm, and I really can't understand why you're upset. Deek is all hot on this Nelson kid. He does all that kinky stuff Deek likes. So you might as well come with me. Crew comes on board a little after dawn, and we sail for the South Seas, three months of sun and tropical islands.... And I'm known for being reasonably generous when I like a young man. You think about it. I've got to get back to the wheelhouse and navigate us to the city. Come on up when you feel sociable... and don't forget to eat. I can hear your stomach growling."

When Quentin had gone Billy picked up the plate and looked at the food. He hadn't eaten all day, except for two cookies and a glass of milk at lunch, when he had been busy cleaning the apartment. Billy did feel a little lightheaded.

"Hey!"

The sharply whispered word made Billy jump. He turned to find Nelson, crouched in the shadow of a bulkhead.

"Commere."

On his guard, Billy moved over to the superstructure from the rail. He didn't want to get too close to Nelson, fearing a trick of some kind.

"Yes?"

"Listen, I don't know what's going on, but they put some crushed up sleeping pills or tranquilizers or something in the drink, and maybe in the food. I don't know."

As Billy stood there amazed, Nelson slipped away, around the far side of the superstructure.

"Hello? Look, I know it's late, but a friend of mine named Billy is with Mr. Jameson. I'd like to talk to him."

The voice on the phone said that Mr. Jameson was out and that Billy was with him, then asked if there was any message.

"No... thanks." Harold hung up the phone, sure now that what Warren had told him was true, not a case of mistaken identity.

He sat unmoving for a while. Then, knowing now that the telephone was not going to ring, Harold felt no need to stay in this apartment. He couldn't believe Billy would return to Jameson. But he had done exactly that.

Harold got up, hardly aware of what he was doing, and went back for the third time this night to the Beacon bar. He wanted noise, people, liquor, not silence, loneliness, and pain.

"Well, rejoining the world, huh?" Quentin asked, seeing Billy coming into the little wheelhouse.

"Yeah," Billy said. "Getting really cold out there, too."

"Thought over about what I said out there?"

"Yeah... and I'm still thinking about it. Sounds real nice, three months in the South Seas.... But frankly, it's hard for me to think about anything right now. I'm really getting kind of tired. Listen, would you mind if I stayed over tonight?"

"Sure, kid. There's only one bunk available, though: mine."

"I guess that's okay," Billy said. "Where's Deek and Nelson?"

"Down in the cabin, playing their games I imagine. You eat any of that food?"

"Every bit," Billy said, "and the drink was just what I needed." He glanced downward as discreetly as possible, to make sure his suitcase was right there at his feet. Reassured, he watched the elaborate and massive structure of lights that was San Francisco. It seemed to be swinging south and east as it increased in size.

"About how much longer?" Billy asked.

"Till we berth? Oh, I guess around midnight. You try and stay awake now. Deek and that kid'll be out of the way and we can have us some fun all by ourselves."

A little after eleven Harold got a seat at the back of the bar. He had already had two fast drinks while standing in the Beacon's Friday night crowd, and now he ordered a third. He still felt stunned, all emotions were on hold, and Harold desperately wanted to knock himself out with bourbon on the rocks tonight before his feelings returned. He knew it would take quite a while, but he had almost three hours to go, and at two o'clock, if he weren't ready to pass out, there was more bourbon at home. And here he had friends. Frank was there behind the bar, and Warren was a few stools away. The Beacon was a good place to be. Only oblivion was better, and with any luck he would be there in a few hours.

Frank thought Harold looked like a dog that had been kicked, then realized his friend was trying to drown himself in booze. Hoping to get him to his own place later, after he got the bar closed up, for some sympathy and understanding, nothing more, Frank began watering Harold's drinks.

Warren, observant as ever, silently rejoiced when he saw Frank, serving Harold, set the drink in front of him, then press his big hand, which until that moment had lain on the bar top as if dead.

"Here we are," Quentin said. "Billy, I want you to tie up. You know that coil of rope at the bow, white and with a big loop in the end?"

"Yeah."

"Well, when we get in toward the berth, you throw it to Nelson. And Nelson, you jump — no, you're still sick."

"Yes."

"Darling," Jameson said, "Nelson and I just smoked some grass, so his stomach is calmed down, but he's rather woozy in any case. I will throw the rope to Billy. Billy, you can jump down to the floating dock, can't you?"

"Uh, yeah."

"Not too tired?" Quentin asked, concerned.

"I can manage," Billy said, then yawned.

"All right, out of the wheelhouse and get ready."

Billy quietly picked up his suitcase and dreamily walked to the bow. As the now suddenly slow-moving craft slid along beside a floating walkway of thick, white painted wooden slats, Billy jumped, suitcase in hand. He landed crookedly, and water sloshed over his ankles for a brief moment before he righted himself.

Above, on the deck of the slow moving yacht, Deek held a mass of rope in his hands. "Catch!" he yelled playfully, amused to be playing sailor.

Billy picked up his suitcase and ran as fast as he could along the planking.

"Billy!" shouted Jameson.

"Come back here!" Quentin roared from up in the wheelhouse.

Billy climbed the dew-damp white wooden stairs that brought him to the flat, dark expanse of the Marina Green.

A loud pop, as of a gunshot, brought Billy to a halt. He turned to see that a long, fence-like stretch of floating dock stuck up into the sky at an odd angle. Realizing the yacht must have run into the docking, and hearing a mass of extremely foul language and now and again his name, Billy ran like hell.

At the Beacon it was nearly one a.m., and most of the men who were interested in pairing off had done so and left. Frank was able to talk for a few minutes with Harold, and his friend had reached the point of wanting to talk about what was on his mind.

"Billy's gone," Harold said. "Back to that Jameson guy.... I don't understand it... everything was fine this morning.... I just don't understand."

"That's why you're trying to get smashed?" Frank asked, his voice all kindness.

"Yeah.... Why did he have to come back and wreck everything? That's what I can't understand."

"He wrecked a lot, maybe, but not everything," Frank said, noting that Harold was too miserable to hear a word.

Billy got the money out of his pocket before the taxi driver stopped. "This corner's fine." Billy paid and got out. He looked up at the windows of his and Hal's apartment. No lights. He looked in the windows of the Beacon bar, just behind him, and he hurried inside.

Frank was glad, when he saw Billy coming in, that the back of the bar had few customers in it besides Warren and Harold, only two guys over at the tables, preparing to leave.

What's that cheap little game-playing hustler up to now, Warren wondered.

Earlier in the evening Harold had wanted to find Billy. More recently he had merely wanted to get his hands on him. And here he was.

Frank got ready for fireworks.

Billy sat down next to Harold, stowing his suitcase at his feet. "Hi. Hoped I'd find you here. I kept trying to phone you.... Harold?"

"I'm listening. Why the hell not? This is the second time you wrecked my life. I don't know where you're going to sleep tonight, but I'll listen to ya."

"Well, okay," Billy said, feeling he was seated next to several hundred pounds of frozen rage that might melt at any moment. "I left my suitcase and some clothes at Deek Jameson's, and I wanted them back, so I called him."

"*You* called *him*," Harold said.

"Right.... Hal, let's talk about it in private."

"Right here's private enough," Hal said.

"Okay.... So I went there, and my clothes were someplace else, and I still thought I could get the luggage and be home before you got back from work, but it didn't come out that way. What happened is this."

Billy told the whole story. At first Frank and Warren pretended not to be listening, but that melted away as their interest in the narrative increased. Harold didn't move, not even to sip at his drink, and he never took his eyes from Billy's face.

When he finished, saying, "...and here I am," there was silence.

"Sounds like you were really close to getting kidnapped," Frank said.

Warren made no comment, but his feelings about Billy had changed a great deal in a short time.

Billy put his hand out to grip Harold's forearm, but Harold pulled away, saying "Okay, ...but all that for a suitcase with some old clothes in it?"

Tired and now angry, Billy snapped, "It had all my stuff in it! Look, I'll show you." He lifted the suitcase up to the bar and opened it. Rummaging down through the clothing, Billy pulled out a ten-by-twelve inch manila envelope that was creased, fuzzy, and dirty with use. He shook out its bulging contents onto the bar top.

"Here, remember this?" Billy asked Harold. "The picture we took at the amusement park back home, in the photo booth when nobody was around, so we could have one together? And these birthday cards from you, and Christmas cards. And here's the ticket stub from the first movie we went to. And look." He held up a matchbook on which was printed the words *Beacon Bar*. "That's from the first night we came here. And there's all this other stuff, some from high school, most of it from back home. I'll show you later if you want to see it."

Embarrassed at displaying his sentimentality so openly, Billy pushed everything back into the envelope. "My birth certificate and those kinds of papers too," he said. "Maybe you think the other stuff is silly, but the official papers are important to have."

"Billy?"

"Yeah, Hal?"

"You scared me to death disappearing like that. But I'm such a shit."

Billy took hold of Harold's forearm, and the two swung together in

126

a deep embrace.

When finally they came apart, Billy said, "I just didn't know what I was getting into. I kind of screwed up, but—"

"Never mind. I screwed up too.... Let's go home."

In a short time Frank and Warren were left alone. Frank took care of a couple of drink orders, then came back to his friend. They looked at each other, both wearing wry smiles.

Warren was the first to speak: "You remember that bet we made?"

"Yeah."

"Well, Frank, I think you won it, really, at last."

"Could be. Those two sure are made for each other, if any two guys are."

"Guess so. Listen, I have a confession to make. I saw Billy in a big limo with a chauffeur this afternoon, and at that time I thought he was, well, a sleazebag, so I told Harold about it. Figured it might help you two to get back together...."

"Not very nice, but under the circumstances—"

"Right, and for a good cause, Frank — you and Harold."

"Mmm.... I noticed you were sort of worrying about me and Hal. Kind of a surprise, if you don't mind my saying."

"Surprised me too," Warren said. "For years everybody in my life has been just another guy. Short, tall, whatever.... Then all this nonsense with those two and — oh, I don't know, I just began to see things in a different light. You, for instance: you're not just another guy, you're Frank .." Warren stopped, feeling a little embarrassed at his words.

"Yeah? I always thought *you* were kind of something extra."

"Thanks," Warren said quietly. "After you close up here, how about breakfast, on me?"

"Sounds good."

"And after that I thought I might ask you up to my place for a drink, of course with the real intention of getting you into bed."

"Yeah? Warren, I thought you were allergic to making it with someone you actually know by name."

"I was. Probably still am, for most people."

"You know you're taking a chance," Frank said. "What if we got a thing going? Wouldn't that hit your panic button?"

Warren got up from his bar stool. "You'll be done here around two-thirty, right?"

"Right."

"Okay, I'll be back with the car. I want to go home and, you know,

127

pick up the dirty socks, change the sheets, like that. . . . Then I'll come back and take that chance you were talking about."

"Sounds good to me," Frank said, watching his friend wave good-night and leave the Beacon. Then he noticed a long envelope lying on the bar top. He picked it up and could feel money inside. Below the names of restaurants and hotels that were written in his own hand he spotted somebody else's script. It read,

A *lot* of thanks to a really great guy.

Billy

THE END

Other ALYSON books you'll enjoy
Don't miss our *free book* offer on the last page

THE BUTTERSCOTCH PRINCE
by Richard Hall; $3.95

Cord and Ellison meet in a theater and are amazed to realize that they look like twins — except that one is black, the other white. When Ellison is found dead in his apartment, Cord takes it upon himself to find the murderer. But he has only one clue; pursuing that clue takes him on some unexpected trips within the New York's gay subculture.

REFLECTIONS OF A ROCK LOBSTER
A story about growing up gay
by Aaron Fricke; $4.95

No one in Cumberland, Rhode Island was surprised when Aaron Fricke showed up at his high school prom with a male date; he had sued his school for the right to do so, and the papers had been full of the news ever since. Yet until his senior year, there would have been nothing to distinguish Aaron Fricke from anyone else his age. You'd never have guessed he was gay — and Aaron did his best to keep it that way.

Now, in *Reflections of a Rock Lobster*, you can read Fricke's moving story about growing up gay — about coming to terms with being different, and a lesson in what gay pride can really mean in a small New England town.

FRANNY: THE QUEEN OF PROVINCETOWN
by John Preston; $3.95

Even if you dressed Franny in leather, he'd still look like a queen. It's the way he walks, his little mannerisms, and his utter unwillingness to change them or hide them that give him away.

And there's something else about Franny. It's a way he has of coming into your life and making his mark on it. As Franny's boys can tell you, once you know the Queen of Provincetown, your life may never be the same.

Most of the books listed here are available in England from Gay Men's Press, PO Box 247, London, N15 6RW.

CHINA HOUSE
by Vincent Lardo; $5.95

If you've been waiting for a good story for a stormy night, one you won't want to put down, here it is. This new novel has all the romance and intrigue you'd hope for in a gay gothic. The author (whose pen name Julian Mark will be familiar to many readers) has created a suspenseful story complete with a deserted New England mansion, a handsome young heir haunted by the death of his twin brother, and a father-son relationship that's closer than most.

QUATREFOIL
by James Barr
introduction by Samuel M. Steward; $6.95

Phillip Froelich is in trouble. The year is 1946, and he's traveling to Seattle where he will face a court-martial for acting insubordinate to a lazy officer in the closing days of World War II. On the way to Seattle he meets Tim Danelaw, and soon the court-martial is among the least of Phillip's concerns...

So begins *Quatrefoil*, a novel originally published in 1950. It marked a milestone in gay writing, with two of the first non-stereotyped gay characters to appear in American fiction. For readers of the Fifties, it was a rare chance to counteract the negative imagery that surrounded them.

Now we have reissued *Quatrefoil*. Readers today will find that it provides a vivid picture of what it was like to be gay in our recent past; on top of that, it's still an entertaining and well-crafted novel.

$TUD
by Phil Andros; $6.95

In the 1960s, while other writers were churning out mass-produced, formula porn, Samuel Steward (under the penname Phil Andros) was different. He was a former English professor and a tattoo artist (trade name: Phil Sparrow); he also had a good sense of humor. All these qualities came together in the Phil Andros stories, which elevated gay erotic writing to a new level. Now we have re-issued *$tud* in a new edition, with an introduction by John Preston. If you remember *$tud* from the sixties you'll be glad to know it's back. If you didn't read it then, you're lucky. You can still read these stories for the first time.

ONE TEENAGER IN TEN
edited by Ann Heron; $3.95

One teenager in ten is gay. Here, 26 young people tell about how they came to discover their homosexuality; about how and whether they told their parents and friends; and what the consequences were.

COMING OUT RIGHT
A handbook for the gay male
by William Hanson and Wes Muchmore; $5.95

Any gay man will have no trouble remembering the first time he stepped inside a gay bar. It's a frightening and difficult step, often representing the transition from a life of secrecy and isolation into a world of unknowns.

That step will be easier for gay men who have read *Coming Out Right*. Here, the many facets of gay life are spelled out for the newcomer: how to meet other gay people; what to expect when going home with a gay man; medical problems you could face; employment opportunities and discrimination; getting insurance for gay couples; what to expect at bars, baths and cruising spots; the unique problems faced by men coming out when they're under 18 or over 30. . . . in short, here in one book is information you would otherwise spend years learning the hard way.

Get this book free!

When were you last outraged by prejudiced media coverage of gay people? Chances are it hasn't been long. *Talk Back!* tells how you, in surprisingly little time, can do something about it.

If you order at least three other books from us, you may request a FREE copy of this important book. (See order form on next page.)

To get these books:

Ask at your favorite bookstore for the books listed here. You may also order by mail. Just fill out the coupon below, or use your own paper if you prefer not to cut up this book.

GET A FREE BOOK! When you order any three books listed here at the regular price, you may request a *free* copy of *Talk Back!*

— — — — — — — — — — — — — — — — — —

Enclosed is $_____ for the following books. (Add $1.00 postage when ordering just one book; if you order two or more, we'll pay the postage.)

☐ The Advocate Guide to Gay Health ($6.95)
    (A complete handbook for men and women)
☐ Butterscotch Prince ($4.95)
☐ China House ($4.95)
☐ Coming Out Right ($5.95)
☐ Death Trick ($5.95)
    (A murder mystery with a gay detective)
☐ A Different Love ($4.95)
☐ Franny: The Queen of Provincetown ($3.95)
☐ One Teenager in Ten ($3.95)
☐ Quatrefoil ($6.95)
☐ Reflections of a Rock Lobster ($4.95)
☐ $tud ($6.95)
☐ Send a free copy of *Talk Back!* as offered above. I have ordered at least three other books.

name: _____

address: _____

city:_____state:_____zip:_____

ALYSON PUBLICATIONS
PO Box 2783, Dept. B-37, Boston, Mass. 02208

This offer expires December 31, 1984. After that date, please write for current catalog.